Mack

The Walkers of Coyote Ridge, 8

STANDALONE NOVELS
Unhinged Trilogy
A Million Tiny Pieces
Inked on Paper
Bad Reputation
Bad Business

NAUGHTY HOLIDAY EDITIONS
2015
2016

Mack

THE WALKERS OF COYOTE RIDGE, 8

NICOLE EDWARDS

Published by Nicole Edwards Limited
PO Box 1086, Pflugerville, Texas 78691

Mack
The Walkers of Coyote Ridge, 8
Nicole Edwards

This is a work of fiction. Names, characters, businesses, places, events and incidents either are the products of the author's imagination or used in a fictitious manner. Any resemblance to actual persons, living or dead, business establishments, events, or locals is entirely coincidental.

COVER DETAILS:
Image: © Wander Aguiar | WanderBookClub.com
Model: Wander Aguiar
Design: © Nicole Edwards Limited

INTERIOR DETAILS:
Formatting: Nicole Edwards Limited
Editing: Blue Otter Editing | BlueOtterEditing.com

ISBN:
Ebook 9781644180143 | Paperback 9781644180136 | Audio 9781644180150

SUBJECTS:
BISAC: FICTION / Romance / Gay
BISAC: FICTION / Romance / General

Dedication

To Happily Ever After.

When you're lucky enough to find it,
grab hold and don't ever let go.

Prologue

Four years ago…

STARING AT HIS PHONE, MICHAEL "MACK" SCHWARTZ felt a cold chill slither down his spine. The kind caused by tragedy, loss, anything that resulted in emotional devastation.

Daniel: *We need to talk. Today.*

"Everything all right?"

Jerking his attention away from the cell, Mack looked up at Jeff, forced a smile. "Yeah. Of course."

Mack could see the doubt, the concern in Jeff's hazel eyes. It seemed to be there all the time now, and Mack wondered if he felt it, too. Something was about to happen, something that would change the course of their lives forever. Which, honestly, sucked major ass, because Mack was too damn old for this shit. Granted, age was merely a number, not a barometer. At fifty-two, he honestly felt as though he'd just started living his life.

With Jeff.

Only shit had gone awry a couple of months ago, back when Mack had stupidly inquired about Alluring Indulgence Resort. He'd been curious, no reason to deny it. And his curiosity had turned out to be the sparks that would soon burn his world to the ground. Since that night at the resort, rumors had begun to spread through Coyote Ridge, rumors claiming Mack and Jeff were together, something they'd done well to hide for the three years they'd been dating.

It wasn't that Mack gave a shit who knew, but he knew they had to keep it on the DL because Jeff was in the public eye, the sheriff of Coyote Ridge. It was an electable position, which meant Jeff had to appeal to the masses or he risked losing the career he'd worked so hard to establish. The thought of Jeff going down in those flames … it caused an ache Mack wasn't sure he could deal with.

"Well, I'll see you tonight," Jeff said softly, stepping toward him.

Mack knew he was waiting for a kiss, so he reluctantly offered one because sending him off into the dangers of his job without it was like telling the man he didn't care, and that couldn't be further from the truth.

After Jeff left for work, Mack locked up the man's house, got in his truck, and headed for Moonshiners. For the first time in a damn long time, he dreaded the thought of going into work. Not only because he knew he would garner a few stares since people were now curious as to what he was doing behind closed doors, but more so because he knew he would have to deal with Daniel. Anytime his son demanded they talk, it never ended well. For the past thirteen years, their relationship had been on rocky ground. Ever since Daniel learned that Mack was gay, a secret Daniel's mother had promised to keep. Not that Mack blamed her for telling the boy the truth. It wasn't her fault even if she'd gone about it the wrong way. In a perfect world, Mack would've been the one to tell him.

But they all knew the world wasn't perfect.

Not even close.

When Mack pulled into Moonshiners, the parking lot was empty as usual this early. He drove through the gravel lot and parked at the back, using the rear entrance to get inside. As he went through, flipping on the lights, his gut tightened into knots. He wanted to call Daniel, to tell the boy he didn't have time to talk tonight, but it would've been a lie, and Mack had made a point not to lie to the kid. Not ever again.

He made a detour into the small office he rarely used, unlocked the safe, and retrieved the cash box he kept inside. He transferred some of the bills to the register he kept beneath the bar, then turned on the credit card machine so it would be ready for the customers once they came in. He was about to head to the stockroom to unload yesterday's delivery when there was a pounding on the front door.

Dread made his stomach churn, but he forced his boots to carry him to the door. Using the key tethered to his belt loop, he unlocked the door, pushed it open. The glare of the setting sun backlit Daniel, casting his face in shadow as the boy stepped inside. Mack didn't need to see his face to know he was angry. It was etched into the tense lines of his shoulders, the clenched fists at his sides.

"Hey," Mack greeted softly, not bothering to lock the door behind him. He got the feeling Daniel wouldn't be staying long.

Daniel spun around to face him. "Why'd you do it?"

Mack stopped, met Daniel's blue stare. "Do what?"

"Make a mockery of yourself?"

The heat in his son's words threatened to singe Mack's beard, but he held his ground. "You'll need to be more specific."

"You think it's funny that the whole town thinks you're an abomination?"

Mack frowned, but his throat was too tight for any words to escape.

Daniel pivoted away from him, marched toward the bar only to stomp back toward him.

"I don't even live here and I'm up to speed on the fact that you're a laughingstock in this town. You and the sheriff, Dad? You just couldn't help yourself, could you? Couldn't simply keep that shit locked up tight. You had to go and let the world know."

Mack's shock turned to anger, but he held on to it. Daniel had every right to be angry with him.

"It ends now," Daniel demanded, his eyes blazing with hatred. "If you want a relationship with me, this bullshit with the sheriff ends now. Tonight."

Mack swallowed past the lump in his throat.

"You owe me this," Daniel insisted. "You lied to me growing up, then I had to hear it from my mother. She didn't bother to sugarcoat her thoughts on it, either, Dad. You're an abomination. Soiled and dirty and you used her."

Used her? Mack was confused. He'd never used Meredith. Granted, he'd done his best to love her, but he'd never been able to do it. Not because she wasn't worthy but because ... because Mack had always known deep down he couldn't love a woman. He wasn't built that way. And yes, he had failed her epically, but he'd done right by his son. Truth was, he loved Daniel more than he loved himself, and the only thing he'd ever wanted was for his son to be happy.

"If you don't end it with him, you'll never see me again," Daniel seethed.

"Daniel, please don't—"

"I mean it. End it with him so this town stops thinkin' you're some sort of deviant, Dad. You owe me that much."

Mack

Inhaling deeply, Mack tried to relax even as his heart constricted in his chest. If he didn't know better, he'd think he was having a heart attack. But this wasn't a cardiac event that could be detected on a machine. After all, broken hearts couldn't be seen on an X-ray or an MRI or whatever machine they used to check out that vital organ.

Daniel took a step closer, locked eyes with Mack. "Prove to me that I mean more to you than anyone else."

"Okay," he said softly.

Daniel's eyes narrowed. "You'll break it off with him?"

"Yes."

"Tonight. I don't want to find out you've spent another night with him, understand?"

Mack nodded.

"But don't think for a second this makes up for the hell you've put me through," Daniel said, his voice rough with his anger.

"I don't," he assured his boy. "And I'm sorry."

"You should be. But I promise, you'll be making this up to me for a long damn time."

It would be years before Mack truly understood how sincere Daniel was about that promise.

Chapter One

Friday, January 17, 2020

"PLEASE TELL ME YOU'VE GIVEN IT SOME thought."

Mack swiped a rag over the bar top as he glanced at his son beneath lowered lashes. Funny, he'd never paid much attention to the many grooves and ridges that had formed in the wood over the years, but they stood out today, felt almost familiar. A small comfort in an otherwise awkward situation, which pretty much summed up all the conversations he'd had with Daniel for the past four years.

"I've been a little busy," he told his son, not bothering to make eye contact.

The boy sighed. "Father, we've talked about this. You know how I feel about you running a bar. It's beneath you, honestly."

Mack did his best not to flinch. He hadn't figured out what was with the whole "father" bit. The kid had called him Dad up until the last couple of years. Then again, Daniel had seemed a relatively normal kid until he'd learned the truth about Mack. After Daniel had suspected Mack was gay, he'd confronted his mother only to learn the cold, hard truth. For the past seventeen years—nearly half Daniel's life—the boy had been harboring a hatred borne of that lie and used it to punish Mack at every turn. As though that hadn't been bad enough, somewhere along the line, Daniel had shed all semblance of normalcy and acted as though he was some high-bred snob.

"You can't even fathom how this reflects on me," Daniel continued. "I can't even tell people about you and I want to, I really do."

Mack sincerely doubted that.

"I think it's time you shed this cowboy crap and moved to the city." The kid added a smile as though that would be the clincher. "I know a great apartment complex right down the street from my work. I'll feel better knowing you're close. That way I can keep an eye on you, help you."

By help, Mack knew his boy meant turn him into someone he wasn't. If Daniel had his way, Mack would be sporting fancy duds with some oblivious woman dangling on his arm.

"My house is paid for," he countered, tucking the rag on a metal hook before flipping on the faucet to wash his hands.

"Exactly my point. You can sell it. I'm not sure you'll get much for it, but what you do get, you can use to pay your rent. Until we find you something else to do. It'll take effort, but I know a guy who can manipulate a resume, make it look like you have worthy skills."

Cut right through the bone, that boy.

"Once you're settled in the city, we can work on your image, get you cleaned up."

Oh, hell. Mack knew what was coming next.

"Once we do that, we'll work on getting you a date. I'm sure there're plenty of single ladies your age."

Yeah, well, there was one major flaw in his son's ill-devised plan. Mack was gay, and no single lady—regardless of age—was going to catch his eye.

"I've considered gettin' a dog," he told Daniel. "Apartments don't allow dogs."

Another sigh. "You don't need a dog, Father. You're getting up there in age, and the last thing you need is someone dependent on you. We both know that's not your strong suit, anyway."

Though both those points rankled, Mack couldn't get past the dig at his age. At fifty-seven, he didn't feel all that old. Well, that wasn't entirely true, but he blamed his overindulgence in booze for that recent development. As of late, he'd established a fondness for whiskey, and he indulged every night.

In his defense, it was the only thing that helped him sleep.

That and his late-night visitor, but Mack couldn't afford to think about Jeff right now. Certainly not with his homophobic, highfalutin son sitting a foot away.

"I tell you what," Daniel said as he got to his feet. "A good friend of mine's a Realtor. I'll reach out to him, get his advice on how we market your house and this bar. I'm sure he knows someone in commercial real estate." Daniel peered around, the flare of his nostrils signaling his distaste for the place Mack considered his home away from home.

Since it wouldn't do any good to argue with the boy, Mack nodded. The familiar flash in Daniel's eyes was like a punch to his solar plexus. The one that said Mack owed him and he would for the rest of his miserable life.

"Hey, Mack. Could I get a beer down here?"

Mack peered down the bar at the big cowboy, nodded.

15

Daniel leaned over. "While we're on the subject of image, I'd really like you to consider going by Michael. Mack's far too redneck for my tastes."

In an effort to hold on to his temper, Mack bit his tongue, nodded again, and he didn't take a full breath until the door closed behind Daniel.

"What in all tarnation was that shit?" Chester Sharpe asked, glaring at Mack.

"It's nothin'," he told his old friend.

"You thinkin' about sellin' this place?"

Ah, hell.

Chester's boisterous voice tended to carry on a good day, and it didn't skip his notice that several people had heard his question, including Travis Walker, who was sitting at a table with his husband and two of his brothers.

When Mack met Travis's concerned gaze, he gave a subtle shake of his head. At this point, Mack hadn't committed to anything, and he wasn't about to get into it with Travis or anyone else.

"And I damn sure ain't gonna call you Michael," Chester snarled before downing the rest of the cheap whiskey in his glass. "That's some bullshit right there."

Doing his best to put that conversation behind him, Mack was grateful when the bar began to fill up. That was the trend. Around eight o'clock on Friday was when the influx occurred, and aside from closing time, it didn't let up until last call on Sunday morning.

"Hey, Mack," Bailey greeted with a beaming smile. "You're lookin' mighty handsome tonight. New shirt?"

"Young lady," he said with a nod, refusing to peer down at his T-shirt. The girl knew damned good and well it wasn't new, but her positivity lightened his mood.

She moved closer to him, still smiling, though he noticed the strain. "You might wanna keep an eye on the pool tables. There's a rowdy bunch back there."

"Yes, ma'am."

As he continued with his duties of pouring drinks and cleaning, he did as Bailey requested, continuing to monitor the situation in the back. The rowdy cowboys weren't anything new, and as long as they kept their ruckus peaceful, Mack didn't do much to interfere. However, he had two rules. First and foremost, those who visited his establishment had to show proper respect to his waitresses. Secondly, he would start knocking heads if and when they didn't. And most folks in Coyote Ridge did not want to see Mack brawl. Hell, it had been years since he'd had to put hands on a patron, and he didn't intend to pick up the habit again.

"Why's that boy so insistent you dump this place?" Chester grumbled, his eyes on the bar in front of him.

Mack didn't answer, hoping the question was rhetorical. He knew if he waited long enough, Chester would come up with an answer.

"Seems like he ain't all that fond of you," Chester said, continuing his monologue. "Ain't got no right waltzin' in here and tryin' to turn you into somethin' you ain't."

"My sentiments exactly."

Mack glanced over, noticed Travis had appeared at the opposite end of the bar. He motioned Mack over.

With a sigh, Mack shifted his feet, cleared the distance between them.

"I don't know what your plans are," Travis told him, his voice low. "But if you're thinkin' of goin' the route that kid of yours wants, I'd appreciate a private conversation with you first."

Mack

Because Mack respected Travis's old man, he gave a curt nod. He figured sooner or later Daniel was going to wear him down. As it was, Mack had gone so far as to peek at real estate in Austin, though it made him cringe whenever he did. But for the past four years, the kid had been chipping away at him, making his life hell with his demands, his constant reminder of what a fuckup Mack had been in the parental department. He'd done it enough, Mack had begun to lose sight of the good times he'd had with the boy, back before his secret slipped out and Daniel had developed a hatred for him.

Mack knew he had to make up for his sins somehow. He'd merely hoped it wouldn't come down to him giving up *everything* he loved, but that did appear to be Daniel's goal.

JEFF ENDSLEY WAS OFF DUTY TONIGHT AND he knew he should've been enjoying himself. He could've caught a movie, gone to dinner, paid a visit to his daughter and grandsons, or sat at home on his ass and read a book.

Aside from visiting his daughter and grandsons, none of those things appealed to him. Since he'd already stopped by Kennedy's twice this week, he risked the chance of overstaying his welcome, so here he was, sitting in his office, taking care of the backlog of paperwork. He was the sheriff of Coyote Ridge, and it was a never-ending cycle, and even though he put in extra hours on his nights off, he couldn't seem to keep up with the influx.

As he stared at the computer monitor in front of him, hen-pecking at the keyboard, he let the police radio fill the silence. He liked keeping up with what was going on in his town. So far tonight, his deputies had dealt with a neighbor complaint, a stray dog digging in someone's garbage, and a couple of hoodlums daring to spray-paint the water tower. The last was a regular occurrence, though Jeff was happy to say, they'd managed to intervene every time for the past three years. The kids these days were a bit more graphic, and the last thing he wanted was Mrs. Whitaker waking up to see a crude image of a cock and balls through her kitchen window. Again.

"All units, be advised we've got multiple reports of a ten-ten in progress at Moonshiners."

Though he should've allowed the deputies to handle the situation, Jeff was on his feet instantly. He snagged his hat from the rack near the door, along with his coat and headed for the parking lot. He didn't bother telling the dispatcher he'd handle it, figuring the closest deputy could deal with the disturbance and Jeff would be there to oversee the situation.

It took roughly three minutes to get from the station to the bar, and by that point, the brawl had spilled out into the parking lot.

Jeff wasn't surprised to see a couple of cowboys throwing down in the headlights from the deputy's car. It used to be a nightly occurrence, but ever since the Walkers had grown up and settled down, it had cooled off some.

"Cassius, I said stop! Don't make me tell you again," Dwayne Downs hollered, his hand on the butt of his gun.

Jeff remained on the perimeter as Dwayne inserted himself between the two pissed-off cowboys. The deputy was intimidating on a good day. Probably had a lot to do with his tremendous size. The man was also damn good at his job, having been working for the department for the past two years.

Jeff kept an eye out to ensure no one was going to spring into action, catch Dwayne off guard.

"You wanna spend the night in a cell?" Dwayne asked Cassius, as out of breath as the brawlers, but his tone was calm and cool.

"No, sir," Cassius snapped, his eyes locked on Rafe Sharpe.

Son of a bitch.

"What about you, Rafe?"

The younger man didn't say a word, fists clenched at his sides.

Jeff wasn't surprised to see Rafe throwing punches. The man had come back to Coyote Ridge only a year ago with a huge chip on his shoulder. It seemed to Jeff he was looking to work off some of the rage he carried around with him thanks to the shitty childhood he and his brother had endured. While his brother, Rex, had learned to live with the ghosts haunting him, Rafe hadn't quite come to terms with his.

"Hey, Mack? You wanna press charges?" Dwayne called out.

Jeff's gaze instantly shot to Mack, who was standing on the wooden porch, hands tucked into the pockets of his jeans.

Speaking of intimidating men… Mack Schwartz didn't have to work to accomplish that feat. He stood six feet tall, and the breadth of his shoulders and chest rivaled Dwayne's. And at fifty-seven, Jeff wouldn't be surprised if the bar owner could hold his own in a knock-down drag-out.

Not that he wanted to see that.

"No," Mack hollered. "But they can cool their jets elsewhere."

Before Mack turned to head back inside, Jeff ensured he saw him. Their eyes locked for long seconds, a silent conversation ensuing before Mack strolled back into the bar.

Never failed, whenever Jeff set eyes on the man, a gaping hole opened in his chest. A dark, empty void where the man used to be. And though Jeff had managed to insert himself back in Mack's life as of late, it wasn't going quite the way he'd hoped.

Didn't mean he wasn't going to continue the pursuit. Jeff wasn't one to avoid an opportunity when it presented itself, and until Mack told him to get lost, he had every intention of finding his way back to the man he loved.

"Hey, Sheriff. How's it goin?" Chester Sharpe slurred, leaning against the hood of Dwayne's cruiser, probably using it to keep himself upright.

"Good, Chester. And you?"

"Oh, same ol', same ol'. You know how it is."

Yes, he did.

"You hear? Mack's talkin' about sellin' this place." A big, meaty hand rose to encompass the wooden structure at Chester's back. "Whaddya think 'bout that?"

Jeff's eyes narrowed as he stared at the sign attached to the wall above the porch. The wooden structure had turned gray with age, much of the wood siding needing to be replaced, yet it seemed fitting somehow. The place was as worn and weathered as its owner but still standing strong.

Mack was going to sell Moonshiners? No fucking way.

"That boy of his came in tonight, said he's talkin' to a Realtor or some shit." Chester smiled, revealing two missing teeth on the lower set. "Said we need to start callin' him Michael." Chester snorted. "Michael. Right."

That familiar ache built in Jeff's chest. Looked as though Daniel Schwartz was still working on his father. He'd been chipping away for the past four years now, trying to turn Mack into … well, honestly, Jeff didn't know what Daniel was hoping to accomplish aside from making his father miserable. Had that been his only goal, he would've accomplished that already.

"Stupid shit, huh?" Chester continued. "I ain't callin' him Michael."

Jeff thought about the times he called Mack by his given name. It was only during intimate moments, those times when Jeff wanted to connect with the man on a much deeper level. He still remembered the look on Mack's face the first time he'd done it. Jeff liked to think that name was only for his use, but as with plenty of things, he was stupid to think so. He had no claims to Mack, even if they'd spent damn near every night in each other's arms since Christmas.

"You have a good night," Jeff told Chester.

"Yes, sir." Chester offered a wave. It took two attempts for him to stand tall, but he managed, stumbling back toward the door.

With a sigh, Jeff turned back to his car. Still another hour before the bar closed down for the night.

Just enough time to go home, shower, and change.

Because closing time was exactly what he was waiting for.

Chapter Two

Saturday, January 18, 2020

"GOOD NIGHT, MACK," BAILEY CALLED OUT AS she headed for the front door.

Mack paused his efforts to restock the small refrigerator beneath the bar, turning his full attention on her. "You want me to walk you to your car?"

"Oh, no." She smiled brightly. "I'm good. But thanks."

He snagged the keys from the hook under the bar and headed toward the doors. It was their nightly ritual. He would offer to walk her to her car, she would decline, and Mack would use the excuse of ensuring the parking lot was cleared out to follow her.

"Why do you bother to ask if you're gonna do it anyway?" Bailey teased, hitching her purse on her shoulder as he stepped out into the chilly January night.

"So you think you've got a choice," he told her.

Bailey laughed. "You're a good man, Mack."

Yeah, he knew that wasn't the case, but he didn't bother to argue. The less this woman knew about the hell that had become his life, the better. In fact, Mack preferred no one in this town knew his business, though that was often easier said than done.

Bailey hit the button to unlock her car. "Can I ask you somethin'?"

Mack narrowed his eyes on her, waited.

"Are you gonna sell the bar?"

He exhaled heavily. "I don't know right now."

She nodded, but he could see the disappointment on her face. Mack would have to talk to any potential buyers, let them know she was the best damn waitress he'd ever had. Hopefully, they'd keep her on long after he was gone.

"Good night," she said softly before getting into her car.

Mack waited for the POS to start up, which it finally did. As she drove out of the lot, he made his way back to the porch, watched until her taillights faded in the distance. As he was turning to head back inside, a pair of headlights came from the opposite direction, then angled toward him. Thanks to the sodium lamp that lit the parking lot, he knew it was one of Coyote Ridge's finest. Probably Dwayne coming to check in, make sure all was quiet now that Mack had closed up for the night.

Hoping the deputy would take a wave as a sufficient response, Mack offered one, then turned to head inside.

The crunch of gravel beneath tires ceased, the night going silent when the engine turned off.

Great.

"Wait up," the voice called from behind him.

Swallowing hard, Mack pivoted around, glared at Jeff, who was dropping his feet to the ground as he exited the vehicle. With a resigned sigh, Mack watched the man sauntering toward him, not a care in the world.

"What're you doin' here?" Mack asked, doing his best not to peer around to ensure no one was lurking. Paranoid was not a good look for him.

Jeff didn't respond, but he did open the door and step back so Mack could go inside.

"We're closed," Mack told him, though he knew the sheriff was aware of that.

Without another word, Jeff took the key ring from Mack's hand, locked the doors from the inside, then passed them back.

Mack wanted to be pissed at the guy, but he couldn't muster the energy. Every single night since their encounter at Alluring Indulgence Resort on Christmas Day—twenty-three days ago—Jeff had been making his late-night appearances. Granted, he'd always come to Mack's house, not the bar, so he couldn't begin to guess why he'd done so tonight.

"I've got shit to do," he told Jeff.

"Don't let me stop you."

Confused and, yes, a bit frustrated, Mack sighed. He headed back to the bar, tucked the keys away, and went to work finishing up his nightly process. Restock the fridge, wipe down the bar, replace the empty kegs, slip any unwashed glassware into the dishwasher. Once he was done with that, he could sweep and mop the floor and be ready to open the doors for business tonight.

While Mack worked through his checklist, Jeff proceeded to flip the chairs up onto the tables, clearing the floor. Mack watched him as he tossed a couple of empties into the trash can as he went.

"Why're you here?" he finally asked, needing to know what Jeff's intentions were.

"To see you." Jeff didn't bother looking his way.

"You know this isn't smart," he told him.

Jeff paused, turned to face him. "Is it true?"

Mack frowned, hand paused with a wineglass he was about to put on the rack behind him. "What?"

"Are you sellin' the bar?"

For fuck's sake.

"So you are?"

Mack set the glass in its appropriate place, then turned back to look at Jeff. "Yeah. I'm sellin'."

Seemingly surprised by his admission, Jeff started toward him. "Why?"

"Makes sense, don't you think? When I'm livin' in Austin, won't need it anymore."

Rather than stop on the other side of the bar, Jeff kept coming at him, joining Mack behind the bar.

"You've given up."

He preferred to think of it as giving in, but hey, either worked. Since it wasn't a question, Mack didn't feel the need to answer. They both knew Daniel would win eventually.

When Jeff finally stopped moving, there was only a breath between them. Mack maintained eye contact, though he would've preferred a quick retreat.

"Why?"

"Why what?" Mack asked.

"Why are—"

Mack cut him off by holding up a hand. "I don't wanna talk about it."

Jeff's head canted slightly. "No?"

"No. But that's not why you're here, is it?"

Jeff stepped closer, crowding him. Instinct had Mack backing up until he hit the counter behind him. As usual, his body heated, warmed from the inside out. His cock thickened behind his zipper, that familiar need flooding his bloodstream despite the fact Mack knew this shouldn't happen.

"You think that's all I want?" Jeff asked.

"It's the only thing I've got left to give," Mack said between clenched teeth.

"Well, in that case…" Jeff's eyes dropped to Mack's mouth. "I'm willin' if you are."

For the first few days after they'd returned to their normal routines when the holidays were over, Mack had considered telling Jeff to stay away from him. Unfortunately, his selfish side had kept him quiet. And every night since, he'd work up a sufficient argument as to why the hell they couldn't do this, but even he didn't believe the nonsense rattling around in his head.

So Mack had given in and he knew tonight would be no different.

"No talkin'," Mack grumbled.

"Only fuckin'?" Jeff countered, his hand slipping beneath the hem of Mack's T-shirt, gripping the waistband of his jeans as he stepped closer.

Mack hissed a breath when Jeff's long, strong fingers dipped into the denim, his knuckles scraping against sensitive skin.

Yeah, this he could do, because they both knew it was going nowhere. Soon enough, Mack would be gone, living a life of torment in a city he had no business being in. Because that was his penance, his just punishment for lying to his son, for leaving Daniel's mother, for not being the father he should've been.

He could make it up to the boy and Daniel had told him exactly how.

Perhaps he would hate himself every single day, but Mack knew he owed the boy, and he would go to the ends of the earth to prove to Daniel that he was the most important thing in his life.

Mack just hated how it was going to play out.

Jeff had purposely come to the bar because it seemed a fitting backdrop for the conversation he'd wanted to have.

However, he realized Mack had no intentions of talking or explaining his irrational thinking. Selling Moonshiners was as idiotic a plan as moving to Austin, but Jeff knew Mack. He would do whatever Daniel wanted, no matter the cost to himself. He'd proven it four years ago when he'd abruptly called a halt to their relationship.

Familiar anger bubbled in his chest, but he shoved it down, choosing to focus on the task at hand.

Flipping open the button on Mack's jeans, Jeff continued to stare into those ocean-blue eyes. Mack never flinched, not even when Jeff eased the zipper down, the *chhh-chhh-chhh* heard over the compressor on the refrigerator kicking on.

He took it as a sign that Mack wasn't pushing him away.

They maintained eye contact as Jeff went to his knees on the foam mat behind the bar. He dragged the denim down Mack's thighs, waiting for him to say something. He would, eventually.

At first, Mack had remained relatively submissive during their interludes, but in the past week, Jeff had noticed he was taking charge once again. It wasn't in Mack's nature to be a passive lover, and Jeff had known it would only be a matter of time before he took the reins. Hence the reason he continued to push the issue, wanting a reaction. Any reaction, didn't matter what. Jeff simply wanted to get a rise out of him. More than the inevitable one, that was.

Mack pulled his T-shirt tight to his body, giving him an unobstructed view as Jeff gripped the smooth, warm flesh that was thickening in his fist.

"Is this what you want?" Jeff asked, an obvious taunt.

"You talk too damn much," Mack hissed, eyes burning with the heat Jeff had always craved. "Shut up and suck me."

Though he wasn't keen on the aggression he felt building inside his lover, Jeff allowed it to play out because it was the only way he could ensure Mack was engaged.

Leaning forward, Jeff licked the swollen head, curled his tongue around the crest, still holding Mack's stare. He didn't take him in his mouth though. Instead, he teased the hard flesh, scraping his teeth along the vein that ran down the thick length.

"Suck me," Mack growled, his free hand snaking into Jeff's hair and latching on.

Heat slammed into him, coiling his insides when Mack jerked him forward, his cock sliding past Jeff's lips.

Of course, he rebelled because that was what they did. These days, it was a constant tug-of-war between the two of them. Jeff knew Mack wouldn't say no to him. Not when it came to this. And it almost didn't matter that Jeff wouldn't get the pleasure of spending time with Mack during daylight hours or out in public. They didn't share meals, no pillow talk or cuddling. They were still as in the closet as they'd been long ago, playing a game that Jeff knew would have devastating results because there would be no winner.

In his defense, Jeff had spent years aching for this man, missing him. For the first year after Mack broke things off, every breath had felt like he'd inhaled glass shards. That pain had eased over time, but not the need. He continued to tell himself he was content with this. That being with Mack was all he cared about. It was a horrible lie, but he hoped with time it would become truth.

"Fuck," Mack hissed as he pulled Jeff's head forward. "Your mouth ... so fuckin' hot."

Jeff allowed Mack to maintain control, filling his mouth and his throat, pushing in deep, retreating. At one point, he had never imagined he would be doing this again, on his knees, worshiping at the feet of the man he loved, Mack's thick cock tunneling in and out of his mouth, his musky scent making him light-headed. He wasn't sure how, but they'd come full circle. Albeit temporarily, and with only one objective, but when Mack unleashed on him the way he was now, Jeff found it difficult to care the road that had led them back here.

"Harder," Mack demanded. "Suck me harder, goddammit."

He fought tooth and nail, never giving Mack exactly what he wanted until he took it. When Mack finally tugged his shirt over his head, dropping it to the bar, Jeff knew he was giving in completely. Mack used both hands to hold Jeff's head, guiding him as he fucked his mouth ruthlessly. The man's ragged breaths and deep groans were music to Jeff's ears, his own cock throbbing.

Mack fisted his hair, jerked his head back. Jeff glared up at him, daring him.

"I'm gonna come in your mouth," Mack growled, his voice gravel-laced and desperate.

Jeff simply waited. Another dare.

A deep rumble sounded in Mack's chest as he drove his hips forward. Jeff sucked him hard, his jaw aching with the effort, but he knew it would be worth it. As the man fucked his face, Jeff waited for him to explode, eager to taste him on his tongue. And when Mack's hips stilled, his cock pulsing, Jeff sucked down every last drop.

"My turn," Mack snarled.

His anger surprised Jeff, but it was emotion, so he didn't retreat. He'd been waiting for this, for Mack to lose that control he used as a lifeline. The man was no more than a shell these days, but even Jeff knew that was a facade. It would only last so long.

Mack fixed his jeans, then gave Jeff's shoulder a gentle nudge. He lost his balance, ended up on his ass, but not for long. A second later, Jeff was flat on his back, the top of his head pressed against a keg hidden beneath the bar while Mack knelt by his legs. The big man roughly tugged his jeans, releasing the button, jerking the zipper, then yanking them down his thighs. When the blessed heat of Mack's mouth enveloped his cock, Jeff hissed.

He didn't bother moving, didn't try to control Mack. He simply let Mack suck him off until he couldn't hold back any longer. When he erupted in Mack's mouth, he did so with a long, low growl.

The sound had barely dissipated when Mack was back on his feet, staring down at him.

"You can see yourself out," Mack said before disappearing altogether.

Yep.

Jeff was getting used to that, too.

Chapter Three

Thursday, January 23, 2020

A FEW DAYS WAS ALL THAT WAS necessary for word to spread like wildfire.

Then again, Mack should've known that it would. Coyote Ridge wasn't a big town. Everyone knew everyone, and the one thing they liked more than their many festivals was the grapevine.

The one good thing about people getting wind of an establishment changing ownership was that they all wanted to stop in, check on the validity of the rumor, spending money in the process. Mack had yet to say a word, deflecting at every turn, but he figured that was about to change since Daniel had sent a text an hour ago letting him know he was coming for a visit with his Realtor friend in tow.

Mack wished like hell he could avoid the situation, but he'd long ago learned how well that turned out. He was in this mess because he'd convinced his ex-wife to keep his secret from his son, and in an effort to defend herself, she'd told Daniel as much. Looking back, he probably should've clued Daniel in himself. Perhaps then the boy wouldn't have been so hard on him.

Oh, who was he kidding? The Daniel Mack knew now was not the same kid he'd spent every other weekend with. Somewhere along the way, the boy had shed his laid-back, all-American skin and turned into a … well, to be honest, he'd turned into an asshole of the highest order.

And yes, Mack loved the boy, would no matter what, but he wasn't sure what had prompted his own flesh and blood to be so damn judgmental, so arrogant, so fucking demanding.

The door opened and Mack felt his shoulders knot as he waited to see the face once the glare from the setting sun disappeared. He relaxed when he realized it wasn't Daniel, but Chester.

After shooting the shit with the cowboys near the door, Chester made his way over, smacked a meaty hand on the bar, and greeted him with a "Hi, how are ya?"

"Good," Mack replied. "What can I get you?"

"It pains me that you have to ask," Chester said, shooting a toothy grin.

Mack poured the man his favored gut-rot whiskey, passed the glass down to him.

The door opened again, muscles tensed then relaxed—not entirely, though—when Travis Walker appeared.

"Mack," the big cowboy greeted with a nod, removing his black Stetson and hanging it on one of the hooks near the door.

"Travis," Mack returned.

They stared at one another for a moment, and Mack knew Travis wasn't there to shoot the shit or to get drunk. He had an ulterior motive, and Mack got the feeling it had to do with the gossip making its way down the line.

Great.

"I'll take a beer. Bottle."

"Sure thing," Mack said quickly.

"My brothers'll be here shortly," Travis said. "Put theirs on my tab."

Fucking lovely. Just what Mack didn't need when Daniel arrived, a nosy Walker clan to overhear a conversation Mack wasn't looking forward to.

After handing Travis a beer, Mack went to the back to grab more to fill the refrigerator. When he returned, he came up short, crate in hand.

Every single one of Travis's brothers were sitting or standing at the bar, all seven of them taking up as much real estate as they could. They'd even managed to convince Chester to take a seat elsewhere, which was saying something considering Chester's ass had worked grooves on that stool over the years.

Hoping no one saw his near fumble, Mack carried the crate to the counter, went to work. He was kneeling behind the bar when he heard the door open, briefly wondered if Curtis was going to show, the cherry on top of the Walker sundae.

He took his time, listening for any sound to clue him in to who had arrived.

Good news, it wasn't Curtis.

Bad news, it was Daniel.

"Where's my father?" Daniel demanded, as though the customers were Mack's personal secretaries.

No one responded, thank God.

Standing to his full height, Mack scanned all the faces until he located his son. He forced a smile, but to maintain it, he had to avoid looking at the two men he'd brought with him.

"Father," Daniel greeted formally. "I'd like you to meet Chris Powell. He's the friend I was telling you about. Chris, this is my father, Michael Schwartz."

Mack kept his hands busy so he didn't have to shake the palm dangling with the request.

Chris reluctantly pulled his hand back, clearly shaken that he'd been left hanging. "It's a pleasure to meet you, Mr. Schwartz. May I call you Michael?"

"He'd prefer it," Daniel answered for him.

A snort sounded from the far end of the bar, but Mack ignored it.

"Michael, I'd like to introduce you to Roy Watson."

Mack nodded at the other man.

"Roy deals with commercial real estate," Daniel explained. "I wanted to see if he could do a market analysis on the place, so we'll have an idea of what we're looking at from a financial perspective."

Mack stared at Daniel, slightly confused by the reference to "we."

"Would you mind if I look around, Mr. Schwartz?" Roy asked.

Mack motioned for the man to do as he pleased. If he was hoping to get a personal tour, he was going to be disappointed.

Chris stepped up to the bar. "Do you happen to have seltzer water?"

Well, of course he had seltzer water. It was a fucking bar.

Not that Mack told him as much. Instead, he grabbed a clean glass, started for ice only to hear Chris decline. Using the sprayer, he filled the glass, passed it over, then glanced at Daniel.

"Nothing for me, but thank you, Father," Daniel said. "I was hoping to borrow your keys so I can take Chris to look at your house."

"Actually," Chris interjected, smiling at Daniel, "I did a market analysis based on the information I obtained online, so it's not necessary just yet." His blond head turned toward Mack. "Once we agree, I'll gladly walk your house and give you my suggestions on what needs to be done for us to get the best possible price for your property."

Mack noticed Travis was listening intently, though he wasn't looking directly at Chris.

"You can see here," Chris explained, laying a manila folder on the bar and opening it, "this is your property, and these are a few that've sold recently in the area."

This time, Travis did show interest, glancing over at the paper, making no effort to pretend he wasn't.

Chris glanced to his left, frowned, then peered over at Daniel.

"Would you mind relocating somewhere else?" Daniel prompted Travis, his voice stern.

"I would, yes," Travis said easily, offering an amused grin. "I'm quite comfortable here."

Son of a bitch. Last thing Mack needed was a pissing contest between Daniel and Travis, and no doubt, it was coming.

"This isn't any concern of yours," Daniel continued, then peered over at Mack. "Father, I think it'd be best if we did this in private."

"I'll take another beer," Sawyer said, drawing Mack's attention.

"Me, too," Brendon called out from farther down. "I can get it myself if you've got other things to deal with."

Mack narrowed his gaze on the man before snagging two more beers from the cold box and passing them down. He didn't bother to remove the caps, simply tossed a bottle opener. He could play this game, too.

"Anyway," Chris noted. "Mr. Schwartz ... Michael." He smiled, flashing pearly whites. "As you can expect from me as your Realtor, I did my due diligence looking into the property values in this town before bringing you the information." His smile fell, but it was clearly for effect. "I'm sad to say that the market's taken a turn in recent months. Not exactly at a high point right now, but Daniel has informed me it's urgent that you sell, so I took that into consideration."

Another snort from down the bar. Brendon or Braydon. Maybe Sawyer.

"I'm not sure you're aware of the resort that's a few miles down the road," Chris said, looking disappointed, "but I believe it's dragging down values in the area. Add to that the fact there isn't much being sold, considering the inconvenience to Austin, we're looking at coming in right under one hundred thousand." His steady gaze lifted. "I'd like you to keep in mind, that's on the high end. Good thing is you own the house outright."

"Why's that a good thing?" Travis asked, shifting his body so he was facing Chris.

The Realtor's eyes widened as he glanced over.

"I'm sorry," Travis said, "it's just I have a great interest in real estate. I'm curious about the process."

That seemed to please Chris immensely, although Mack knew it was a load of horse shit. Travis Walker likely had more real estate experience in his little finger than this Chris character did in his whole body.

Another glimpse of Chris's bright white teeth. "In my experience, sir, when a seller owns the property outright, there's more room to play with the numbers."

"How so?" Travis asked, sounding as though he had no idea how it worked.

"Well, in Michael's case, we can——"

"Mack," Travis interrupted.

Chris's perfectly groomed eyebrows rose. "I'm sorry?"

"His name's Mack."

Daniel leaned forward. "He's no longer using that nickname. Unlike the rest of you, he's evolved."

"Ah." Travis nodded as though that made sense. "I guess I didn't get that memo."

Sawyer leaned forward. "You know, Trav, that's probably because you've been too busy runnin' that resort on the edge of town."

A wicked smile formed on Travis's face. "Right. The one bringing down the property values."

Chris glanced over at Daniel. "I'm really not sure what's going on here."

Daniel cleared his throat, turned his attention to Mack.

Knowing this was only going to go downhill from here, Mack offered a tight smile, then marched into the back. Alone.

"HEY, SHERIFF, YOU HEAR WHAT'S GOIN' ON over at Moonshiners?"

Jeff peered up from his computer monitor, pinned his gaze on Dwayne. "What?"

"Word is, Mack's kid brought some real estate boys in. They're lookin' over the place."

Though this bothered him on a personal level, Jeff wasn't sure why it was newsworthy for the sheriff. He'd long ago learned to separate business from pleasure, a necessity in maintaining order in this town.

Dwayne smiled. "That's not the important part."

With a slow exhale, Jeff leaned back in his chair, gripped the arms and tapped his index fingers. That was the one thing about Dwayne: it took him some time to get to the point, but eventually he would arrive at it.

"The Walkers are all headin' up there. Travis's instruction."

"All of 'em?"

"Yup. I'm thinkin' Travis is lookin' to interfere. Think I should head over there?"

Jeff got to his feet. "Naw. I was gonna grab a bite anyway. I'll stop in, see what's goin' on."

Dwayne nodded. "You need any help, just holler."

Without haste, Jeff grabbed his coat and hat, headed out to his cruiser. A few minutes later, he was pulling into the Moonshiners parking lot, only to realize there wasn't a parking space to be had. Looked as though more than just the Walkers were checking out the out-of-towners. Depending on the topic of conversation, that could be good or bad. Because his daughter had married into the Walker family, Jeff had spent plenty of time in their company over the last few years. He knew deep down that the boys' intentions were generally good, even if their methods weren't always appropriate.

After snagging his hat from the passenger seat, Jeff exited his vehicle, settled it on his head, and started toward the door only to be intercepted by Kaden and Keegan Walker, who strolled around the side of the building.

"Hey, Sheriff," Keegan greeted with a shit-eating grin.

"Boys," he acknowledged the pair.

"Headin' inside?" Kaden asked, his tone polite as ever.

"I am."

"We'll follow you," Keegan noted, motioning for Jeff to precede him.

Mack

Kaden kindly opened the door, flashed a brilliant smile as he held it for him. When Jeff stepped inside, the first thing he noticed was the small bar was packed to the gills, most definitely over capacity.

Second was that everyone was silent, with the exception of Daniel and another man at the bar.

Third was that Mack was nowhere in sight.

"Hey, Sheriff," Kaleb greeted from behind the bar. "Can I get you somethin'?"

"When'd you take up bartending?" he asked casually, noticing how all eyes had shifted to him.

"Hobby," Kaleb said, then nodded his head toward the door behind him. "Mack's takin' a break."

"Is there a problem, Sheriff?" Daniel asked when Jeff approached the bar.

"Just stoppin' in to check on things," he said, though he wasn't keen on explaining himself to the man.

Daniel turned to face him. "Michael's just getting something. He'll be back in a minute."

Michael, huh? So it hadn't just been Chester's drunken ramblings.

"I'll just go talk to him," Jeff told the man.

In a move Jeff didn't approve of, Daniel sidestepped, cutting him off.

"I'd prefer if you didn't, sir."

Jeff raised his eyebrows and stared back at the younger man. "Is that right?"

"My father's not accepting visitors."

Several snorts erupted through the room.

"Why don't I determine that for myself," Jeff told him as he stepped to the side.

"Mr. Endsley, I'd prefer you didn't. It's not appropriate."

Only because he was curious as to Daniel's reasons, Jeff paused. "And why's that?"

"I don't think you want me to explain that here," the kid said, his voice lower than before.

A few years ago, Jeff would've agreed with him. Back before his sexual orientation had become public record. In the time since that secret leaked, Jeff had learned to embrace who he was. Had taken far too long, as far as he was concerned, but he owed his newfound respect for himself to those in this town who'd stood up for themselves in recent years. Namely people like Ethan Walker, who'd gone through far more than any young man should have because of who he was. Jeff respected Ethan too much to let his sacrifices go by the wayside.

Irritated now, Jeff turned to face him. "Explain what?"

Daniel stepped forward, lowered his voice. "About your inappropriate relationships."

The door to the bar opened and footsteps sounded from behind him, but Jeff didn't bother to look to see who it was.

"I'm not sure I understand," Jeff told him, wanting to see if the boy would out his father when his disapproval was so evident.

"Sheriff, I think he's sayin' you're gay."

Jeff grinned but didn't look away from Daniel. "Thanks for makin' that clear, Beau."

"No worries," the man called back. "Just doin' my civic duty."

There was some laughter to follow.

"Is that what you're referrin' to?" Jeff asked. "The fact that I'm gay?"

Daniel's eyes widened. Clearly he hadn't expected Jeff to admit it.

"Don't worry, the cat's been outta that closet for a long time," he assured Daniel. "Now, if you'd excuse me, I'm gonna check on Mack."

As chatter sounded behind him, Jeff continued toward the door leading to the stockroom. To ensure their privacy, he closed and locked it behind him before making his way through the rows of shelves that housed bottles and glasses. He stepped around a few empty crates littering the floor.

"Mack?"

A heavy sigh alerted him to Mack's presence. Jeff followed the sound, finding Mack sitting on an old wine barrel, elbows propped on his thighs, staring down at his hands.

"You all right?"

"That's a damn good question," Mack said, though he didn't bother to look up. "I assume you came to see what the ruckus was all about."

"Me and everyone else in town," Jeff answered. "So, is it true? Are you sellin'?"

Tortured blue eyes finally lifted, and Jeff felt a tug somewhere in the center of his chest.

"You can talk to me, Mack," he said softly. "Regardless of what's goin' on between us, I'm still your friend."

Mack seemed to consider that for a minute before he sighed again. "Friends, huh?"

Oh, he wanted more than that, but now wasn't the time and this certainly wasn't the place for that conversation, so Jeff simply nodded.

They remained like that for what felt like an eternity, eyes locked, emotions being held back.

"I've actually been thinkin' it over," Mack told him. "And Daniel's right."

"About?"

"Everything."

So they were back to that. The last conversation they'd had the night Mack had turned Jeff's world upside down had revolved around Daniel being right. Mack had declared that night that he owed his son and he would do anything the boy wanted because Mack's one and only objective in life was to make his son happy. Even at his own expense.

"And yes, I've decided to sell. The house, the bar. All of it."

While that was what Jeff had expected him to say, it wasn't what he'd hoped to hear.

Mack got to his feet. "I know why Travis did this."

"To show you he supports you?" Jeff quipped, trying to wrangle the anger and pain.

"He's hopin' to intimidate me," Mack answered.

"I don't think that's his reason."

"He shows up here, brings half the damn town because he knew my son was gonna be here," Mack argued. "I don't need Travis's help. Hell, I don't need anyone's help."

"They're here to support you," Jeff said firmly. "Not to intimidate you. Or Daniel, for that matter."

Not that they could intimidate Mack's son. Daniel was too oblivious for that.

"So why are *you* here?" Mack asked.

"To check on you," he admitted. After all, it was the truth. If Jeff thought for a second he could intervene, he would. But he knew better than that. He hadn't been able to penetrate Mack's hard shell in weeks, and he knew it wasn't going to happen now, either.

Mack

"You're only makin' it worse, Jeff. You know how my son feels about…"

"About me?" Jeff prompted.

"About my past," Mack clarified.

Jeff had to laugh at that, though he wasn't the least bit amused. "By past, you're referrin' to what we did last night, right?"

And every night for the past month.

"That can't happen again," Mack growled, his voice low. "I tell you every damn time that we can't keep this up."

His fury ignited. "No, Mack. You don't. And if I recall correctly"—Jeff stepped forward, bringing them nose to nose—"you weren't pushin' me away when you were buried in my ass last night."

Mack didn't budge, but his blue eyes glowed with his anger. "It won't happen again, I promise you that."

Oh, hell no. Jeff wasn't going to let him call it off this time.

"You're wrong about that," he said softly, maintaining eye contact. "In fact, you're wrong about every damn thing."

"I'm sellin' the bar, movin' to Austin," Mack hissed. "And you have no say in it."

"Maybe not, but that doesn't mean I'll give up."

Mack barked a laugh. "Give up on what? This ridiculous thing we've got goin'?" Mack's teeth clenched. "It's called fucking, Jeff. And it's over."

44

Rather than counter with words, Jeff did something that surprised them both. He gripped Mack's head and brought their lips together. Mack fought him for a fraction of a second, but then the kiss exploded. Mack's hand fisted in the front of his shirt, jerking him closer. Jeff held him there, tongues dueling, bodies colliding. He heard Mack's ragged breaths and knew they were spurred more by emotion than action. He was barely holding himself together even though he wanted everyone else to think otherwise.

Jeff knew him better than most, though. He knew deep down, Mack carried the weight of the world, and he honestly believed self-sacrifice was the answer to his son's desperate need for happiness.

"I'm not lettin' you do this again," Jeff breathed against his lips. "And that's *my* promise."

"It's not up to you," Mack finally said, his voice hoarse and uneven.

Jeff's heart clenched tightly in his chest. "Maybe not. But it's not up to Daniel, either."

Mack released his death grip and stepped back. Jeff smoothed out his shirt, never looking away.

"I let you walk away before," he told the other man, "and I was wrong. I thought you'd come around. You didn't. But you can't tell me you stopped lovin' me."

Mack's blue eyes remained on his, his pain evident.

"That's what I thought."

Jeff righted his hat, then turned to head back to the bar.

"I'm not through with you, Mack. Not by a long shot."

Mack

"HEY, REESE, YOU GOT A MINUTE?" TRAVIS asked when Reese Tavoularis answered his call later that night.

"Always for you, boss man. What's up?"

"I need a favor."

Reese chuckled. "A favor? Don't you owe me a few dozen already?"

Travis smiled. "One day I figure you'll call in your markers and I'll be here to answer."

"I'm gonna hold you to it."

Travis knew he would. One day. Until then, he did need Reese's help.

"I need you to dig up some information," Travis explained. "Guy named Daniel Schwartz. I want to know every fucking thing there is to know about him. Most importantly, everything he's been up to for the past five years or so."

"Daniel Schwartz?" Reese asked. "This is Mack's kid?"

"Yep."

"Does the craggy bastard know you're diggin' into his kid's life?"

Of course he didn't, because Travis wasn't that stupid. He respected Mack, but that didn't mean he wasn't above risking the man's wrath if it meant figuring out what was motivating the kid to be a royal pain in the ass.

"I'll take that as a no." Reese's resigned sigh sounded. "Am I lookin' for somethin' specific?"

"I'm not exactly sure," Travis told him, though it was only a partial truth. Travis had his suspicions, but until he had some concrete evidence, he didn't intend to start rumors. "But I wanna know everything. Who he's dated, what his favorite restaurant is, how much time he spends with his mother."

"So personal details?"

"Exactly."

"You have a timeframe for this?"

"Yesterday."

Reese laughed. "Always with the ASAP. Couldn't give me a month's notice, could ya?"

"What would be the fun in that?" Travis countered, grinning.

"I'll get right on it, boss man."

"Thanks, Reese. I owe you one."

"Many, Walker. You owe me *many.*"

Travis chuckled as he disconnected the call and set his cell phone on the end table.

"Do I even want to know what you're up to?" Gage inquired as he stared back at him from his seat on the opposite end of the couch.

"Probably not."

Gage shook his head. "I don't think Mack'll appreciate you interferin' in his life."

"That's too fuckin' bad," Travis grumbled. "Man might not think so, but I consider him a friend. And this shit has gone on long enough."

"By shit, you mean Daniel's efforts to turn Mack into some uppity city asshole?"

"Straight asshole, at that." Perhaps that was what irked Travis the most. He'd been as shocked as everyone else when he learned Mack was gay. Unfortunately, the man's personal life had been outed back when AI first opened. Though he'd had no control over that, Travis still felt somewhat responsible. Not that he gave two shits as to who Mack spent his time with. When he'd learned the bar owner and the sheriff were an item … well, he might've said an *atta boy* or something along those lines. Of course, by the time word got out, that relationship had caught fire and burned to the ground. And Travis had spent far too long watching that young fuck of a kid put his old man through the ringer. As far as Travis was concerned, if Mack wasn't going to stand up for himself, someone had to.

"You know I could handle that for you," Gage offered. "I possess some mad computer skills."

That he did, among many, many others.

Mad skills. Oh, yeah.

Images of what they'd done right here on this couch an hour ago flashed in his head, making his body harden all over again.

Forcing the thoughts away, Travis peered over at his husband. "I need you to do somethin' else for me."

"What's that?" Gage smirked, his eyes slowly gliding down to Travis's lap.

"Oh, that's certainly on the agenda," Travis assured him. "Tonight. Right now, I need you to have some papers drawn up."

"For?"

Travis glanced back at the television. "If Mack does sell the bar, I fully intend to acquire it before it makes it to market. Put together a cash offer. Thirty percent higher than whatever they list it for. But you cut that fucking real estate asshole out of it."

Gage nodded. "Will do. You know he might turn you down no matter what."

"Might," Travis agreed. "Highly unlikely, but possible."

However, he hoped it never came to that.

Chapter Four

SO MUCH FOR PROVING HIMSELF, MACK THOUGHT as he sat in his living room on Friday afternoon, trying to find the energy to get off the couch so he could head up to the bar, knock out his opening checklist.

Unfortunately, he couldn't find the energy to do that much, and considering that had been the only thing he'd had to look forward to these past few years, Mack wondered if this wasn't the depression taking over his entire existence.

Not that he really needed to go to work. If he wanted, he could simply shut the place down and let it rot. Rather than go through the hassle of selling, he could simply strike a match and watch it burn. Daniel would be happy if he did. And the town … well, fuck them all. They didn't understand why Mack had to do right by his son. Then again, most of them didn't have children they'd let down in a remarkable way. But that was how Mack rolled. He could disappoint Daniel without much effort.

Sometimes he wondered if he was disappointing his son simply by breathing. Didn't matter how many things Mack did, how many changes he made at Daniel's request, there was always one more.

Dump the man you love. Check.

Don't be gay. Facade in place.

Sell your house. Done. Don't need it anyway.

Sell the bar. Sure, why the hell not?

Move to Austin. Of course.

Live under my thumb. Be happy to.

Fall in love with a woman. Yeah … no.

That wasn't going to happen no matter what Daniel said, but there was no sense in beating a dead horse. As long as Mack pretended to put forth the effort, surely Daniel would be content.

Then again, that was what Mack had thought when he'd ended things with Jeff four years ago, eliminating every ounce of happiness from his life in an effort to appease the son who was embarrassed by him. He hadn't hesitated to cut off his own nose to spite his face.

And here he was, gearing up to add to that list.

Chris, Daniel's Realtor friend, had dropped by an hour ago with a buyer's agreement and a sign for Mack's yard, along with a list of things he suggested Mack do to make the house more appealing. The kid was off his fucking rocker if he thought Mack was going to replace the countertops in the kitchen. Or the appliances. Not for the lame-ass price he was going to get for the place. Shit, he'd probably make more if the house was leveled in a natural disaster.

But the sale of the house wasn't what was bothering him. Truth was, he didn't much give a damn anymore.

No, his irritation was with Jeff. For the first time since Christmas, the man hadn't strong-armed him last night. He didn't show up after closing and he didn't wander over to Mack's once he was home. The sheriff was MIA though he'd promised he was going to prove himself.

Staring at the crack in the wall—the one that had grown over the past few years as it worked its way down from the corner of the popcorn ceiling—Mack wondered at what point he'd started believing Jeff actually owed him anything. The man didn't have to prove himself, because he'd never done anything wrong. Nothing except love Mack, that was.

Yet, from out of the bleak, dark hole in his chest, a bubble of hope had formed that night at the resort when Jeff had insisted they talk. The best Christmas present he'd gotten in years. Not much had been said that night, but it was one Mack would likely remember for the rest of his cold, lonely days. The ones he would spend sitting in some modern, white-walled tomb in Austin while he twiddled his fucking thumbs and waited for Daniel to confirm what he could have for dinner that night.

God, he was tired.

Somehow he found the energy to get to his feet. He headed for the pink-tiled bathroom that he hated with a passion. He pulled back the utilitarian white shower curtain, turned the ancient faucet to start the water, then pulled the knob to transfer it to the shower head. A minute later, he was under the spray, going through the motions. In five minutes flat, he was out and dried off, towel wrapped around his hips while he ran a comb through his hair and his beard. Mack paid little attention to his appearance these days because he couldn't see the point, but he did his best not to look homeless. Once that happened, he figured all was lost.

He took the time to brush his teeth, gargle mouthwash, and wipe his mouth before he headed for his room. The house was so old there wasn't a master bedroom or an en suite, just three small rooms with three equally small closets. The extra rooms he used as storage for shit he'd acquired over the years and a few of Daniel's old things from when he'd stayed on the weekends when he was a kid. Those days were long gone now, his boy grown and living his own life.

Funny, Mack would've figured Daniel would be too busy with his social life to worry about what Mack did, but for the past four years—ever since Mack ended things with Jeff—the kid seemed to have more time on his hands. From time to time they would meet for dinner, but always just the two of them and never in Coyote Ridge.

Mack opened his closet, grabbed the string to turn on the single bulb mounted to the ceiling, then rummaged through the plethora of T-shirts he owned. He had one in every color and seven pairs of jeans, a couple that had seen better days. He blindly grabbed one of each, snagged his black boots from the rack on the floor, then headed back out, tossed his bounty on the bed.

Why hadn't Daniel ever introduced him to one of his female friends, Mack wondered. There was one Daniel had talked about for a while, though Mack couldn't remember her name. Then again, he wasn't sure Daniel had ever told him.

"Probably doesn't trust me," Mack muttered as he retrieved his belt from the top drawer of his old dresser, threw it on the bed.

Yeah, that was likely it. Daniel didn't trust him, but Mack couldn't blame him. He'd lied to the boy for a good part of his life, always deflecting when Daniel inquired as to why Mack's marriage to his mother had gone south. He remembered the fear he'd harbored those days. Every time he went to pick Daniel up at his mother's, he'd expected the kid to know that Mack was at fault because he'd never actually been in love with Meredith though he'd fathered a child with her.

"All my fault," he grumbled, once more accepting the blame.

It was, after all, true.

JEFF STOOD IN THE DOORWAY, WATCHING MACK wander around his bedroom, listening to him mumble to himself as he was known to do. He knew the man had no idea he was there, but Jeff didn't bother to announce his presence, instead taking a moment to observe him in his element.

It pained him to see Mack so down. While he'd never been called a happy man, Jeff had seen him at his best. That smile he rarely flashed used to be what Jeff looked forward to most when he saw him.

"All my fault," Mack repeated, dropping his head as he stood beside the bed.

"What's your fault?" Jeff asked, though he already knew the answer.

Mack spun around so fast the towel around his hips came loose, falling to the floor.

"Leave it," Jeff commanded when Mack reached down for it.

As usual, Mack ignored him, snagging the towel from the floor, but rather than put it in place, he let it dangle from his hand.

Jeff took a step forward, openly ogling the big man.

"What do you want, Jeff?"

He lifted his eyes to Mack's face. "For starters, dinner. Then you. Maybe some dessert afterwards. Then you again."

Jeff loved the way Mack's eyes lost the anger and desolation as they filled with heat. It never had taken much to get him worked up, though there was something lacking in those pretty blue eyes. The warmth that had once been there was long gone, replaced with a gloomy resignation, storm clouds dulling the brilliant shine.

"Honestly," Jeff told him, "I didn't have an agenda. Well, aside from dinner because I picked it up. I simply wanted to see you."

Jeff loved the way Mack's entire face softened, as though he'd needed to hear those exact words. He'd made a point of telling Mack how he felt back when they'd been together because he'd sensed his vulnerability. Mack had never been comfortable in his own skin, racked with self-doubts, and Jeff knew those had grown tenfold over the past few years. Expected with Daniel dogging him at every turn, pinpointing all the things he felt were flaws in his father.

Problem was, what Daniel saw as flaws, Jeff saw as highlights. He'd never wanted to change a thing about Mack, though he knew Mack was always waiting for it.

"I have to go to work," Mack said, his chest muscles flexing.

His pecs weren't the only things hardening on his body though. Seemed Mack still enjoyed Jeff ogling him.

"Actually, you've got the night off. I called Rafe, asked him to fill in. He was only too happy to oblige."

"So, what? You think you can come in and rearrange my schedule for me?"

Jeff locked eyes with Mack. "Not at all. If I did, I'd probably need to get in touch with Daniel. He's the one in charge of it now, isn't he?"

"Fuck you," Mack rasped, turning away from him.

Before he could reach for his clothes, Jeff moved up behind him, took hold of his wrists, and held him in place.

He noticed the subtle tremble under Mack's skin. Anger over Jeff showing up unannounced? Frustration with Daniel? Or was it merely everything coming to a head, the emotion desperate to get out of the bottle Mack had locked it in?

Because he couldn't resist, Jeff pressed his lips to Mack's shoulder, inhaled the spicy scent he'd always loved. "I'm serious about dinner."

"I can't go to dinner with you," Mack said, his tone losing its edge.

"But you can *have* dinner with me. I told you, I already picked it up." He kissed Mack's other shoulder, trying to keep the move casual, though it wasn't easy when Mack was standing so beautifully naked before him.

Mack didn't move.

"You get dressed. I'll set up the food. Join me when you're ready."

"Why don't you just fuck me now. Get it over with so you can leave."

Jeff frowned, releasing his grip on Mack's wrists. "I'm not here to fuck you."

Mack's head fell forward. "That's all I'm good for, Jeff. If I was a stronger man, I'd push you away, make you leave. But I'm not."

Flattening his palms on Mack's smooth, muscled back, he ran his fingers over warm skin.

"This is wrong," Mack whispered. "You know it as well as I do. And it's temporary. Don't tell me you've suddenly accepted a happily never after."

Jeff didn't think of this as temporary, but he wasn't going to argue. Mack had already made up his mind. The proof was staked in the front yard, the For Sale sign a shining beacon of Mack's defeat.

"Have dinner with me," Jeff said softly, then stepped away, leaving Mack in his bedroom to get dressed.

By the time he had the food set up on the table, two glasses of wine added, Mack appeared wearing the charcoal-gray T-shirt Jeff loved. It was old and worn, thinning in some spots. Jeff liked it because it reminded him of the man. That and it brought out the gray in Mack's beard, the blue of his eyes.

"Are you on call?" Mack asked as he pulled out a chair, the legs scraping over the tattered and peeling linoleum.

"Not tonight."

Jeff sat, picked up his fork, and realized Mack wasn't making a move to eat.

"It's your favorite," he said, as though Mack couldn't see the chicken fried steak, mashed potatoes, and green beans Jeff had picked up at the diner in town.

When Mack's gaze lifted, his eyes were stormy with emotion, and it nearly knocked Jeff out of his chair.

"I can't do this," Mack whispered. "I can't."

Jeff didn't ask what he was referring to. It could've been a number of things, but he got the feeling it was a general statement. Partially directed at him for attempting to turn this into something more, partially in reference to what his own son was putting him through.

Didn't matter the reason, because Jeff could hear the truth in those words. The man he'd loved for as long as he could remember was hurting, and it pained him to see it.

Rather than force the issue or try to dig into Mack's psyche, Jeff put his fork down and stood. He walked around the table, took Mack's hand, and tugged him to his feet. A few minutes later, they were lying in Mack's bed, fully dressed. Jeff spooned behind him, arm draped over Mack's ribs.

He pressed a kiss to the back of Mack's neck and kept quiet. Sleep was what Mack really needed. Perhaps once he'd gotten a few hours of shut-eye, they'd be able to hash this out.

Mack

If not, well, there was always tomorrow.

Chapter Five

MACK WOKE IN HIS DARKENED BEDROOM, A warm body behind him. He knew who it was from touch alone, but even if Jeff hadn't been wrapped around him, Mack would've known anyway. He'd always been able to sense Jeff, and right now, he knew he was awake, which was the reason Mack didn't move, just let Jeff's warmth seep into him. He couldn't remember the last time he'd slept so peacefully. Probably not since he'd shared a bed with Jeff years ago.

God, he'd missed this. Being held, loved, protected. He'd spent years feeling as though he was floundering on his own, no roots, nothing to look forward to. And it was all because he'd lost this. The man he loved. In an effort to make up for his sins, Mack had forsaken his own happiness, though these days he couldn't help wondering why he'd been so stupid. No matter how hard he tried, he clearly couldn't make up for failing Daniel, and the more he tried, the more pieces of himself he lost.

"You awake?" Jeff's voice drifted from behind him, the sexy sound rough from sleep.

"Yeah."

When Jeff's hand slipped beneath his T-shirt, gliding over his stomach, Mack covered it with his own, holding tight, never wanting to let go. He loved the way Jeff's fingers spread wide, covering as much as he could. There was no teasing, just comfort, and Mack needed that more than anything. After a few minutes, Mack rolled to his back, giving him better access to whatever he wanted, because Mack had never been able to be in bed with the man and not want more.

Jeff propped up on his elbow, stared down at him.

"Don't stop touching me," Mack whispered, trying to make out Jeff's face in the dark. "I need you to touch me."

"I'll touch you for as long as you'll let me."

The promise in those words had Mack's heart picking up speed. In an effort to help him out, Mack tugged his shirt off, tossed it to the floor. He didn't care how far this went, he simply wanted Jeff's fingers on his skin, something to anchor him for a little while. He felt adrift, racked with pain and anger, defeated in every way. But these past few weeks, he'd felt whole when Jeff was with him, even if for only those few minutes they'd stolen together.

"Feels like just yesterday we were doing this," Mack said as Jeff's lips dropped to his collarbone, his hand gliding over Mack's skin. He inhaled deeply when Jeff's fingers twined in his chest hair, tugging gently. For some reason, he'd always found that simple gesture erotic.

"We probably were," Jeff said with a chuckle.

"Not like this we weren't." He cupped Jeff's head gently, ran his fingers through his soft hair. For too long, he'd missed this. Not only Jeff's touch but the feelings he instilled. The warmth, comfort.

Mack arched his back when Jeff's teeth scraped over his nipple.

"Do that again," he urged.

Jeff continued the sensual torment for several minutes while Mack's body pulled taut. He closed his eyes, focused on the soft rasp of Jeff's breaths, the heat of his mouth.

"Come here," Mack told him, needing to taste his kiss, to feel his lips on his.

In one easy movement, Jeff was covering him. Mack slid his hands over Jeff's back, held him in place, getting accustomed to the familiar weight. While Jeff wasn't a small man, he was considerably smaller than Mack. At least in the weight department. Jeff was lean and trim with the body of a runner, while Mack had been born with bulk, something he'd never been able to shed. By the time he'd been in high school, he had realized his size equated to power, and by honing his muscles, he'd grown into his nickname.

Mack could've spent hours just like this, their tongues mingling, bodies grinding. He worked his hands into Jeff's jeans, cupped his ass, and pulled his hips forward. They rocked together, the friction on his cock making his head spin. He remembered so vividly the mornings he would wake up in Jeff's bed, touching, tasting, exploring just like this. No time limits, no worries, just the two of them. They'd been together for three years, yet the passion had never died. Even now, after so long apart, it was still as it had once been, potent and easy.

When Jeff started to pull away, Mack held him firmly in place, squeezing his ass, not wanting to let go.

"Let me love you," Jeff whispered. "Let me *make* love to you."

Mack swallowed hard, reluctantly releasing his hold so Jeff had the freedom to explore.

"I've missed this," Jeff said softly, his lips sliding along his collarbone, his shoulder, down his bicep.

"I've missed *you*," Mack admitted, though he wasn't sure he said the words aloud.

He surrendered to Jeff, focusing on the feel of his hands, the glide of his lips, the gentle nip of his teeth. His breaths became raspier as Jeff continued his ministrations, eventually working Mack's jeans and underwear off, leaving him naked and vulnerable.

There was no aggression, no anger. Mack had known some of their recent encounters had been more about payback than anything else, a way for Jeff to punish him for what he'd done. The man was good at angry sex, but he was so fucking much better at this.

"Ah, Christ," Mack bellowed, hips lifting off the bed when Jeff took his cock in his mouth.

He squinted, wishing he could see in the dark, wanting to memorize this moment for eternity, to remember what it was like to love and be loved, because God only knew, once he left Coyote Ridge, he would never have this again.

Mack found it difficult to concentrate with Jeff's mouth on him, so warm and reverent as he licked and sucked. Jeff's hands skimmed over his thighs, down to his knees, back up. Those deft fingers teased the sensitive flesh near his groin, higher over his stomach, his chest. The sensation of touch mixed with the warmth of Jeff's mouth had him soaring.

"I want to taste you," Mack told him, cupping Jeff's head, urging him to give him that opportunity.

Jeff lifted his head, and then there was movement on the bed, a dip in the mattress when Jeff slipped off, another when he returned.

Unable to remain still any longer, Mack sat up, pulling Jeff to him, then urging him onto his back. Jeff lay across the bed now, as Mack hovered over him, turning around and straddling Jeff's head while his lips hovered over the man's rock-hard erection. He let his breath fan over the rigid length before sliding his tongue along Jeff's shaft. Soft moans sounded from both of them when Jeff took Mack's cock between his lips once more.

And then there was nothing but sensation as Mack relished the feel of Jeff's cock in his mouth while the man's lips and tongue did the same in return. Long minutes passed, but neither was working toward the end goal, merely filling time, loving one another in the one way they'd always been good at.

Mack wanted it to last forever, needed the memory to sustain him when this was no longer an option.

A moment he feared was coming far too soon.

———

JEFF COULD FEEL THE DIFFERENCE IN MACK. From the moment he'd woken up, he'd sensed the old Mack was with him, the one who loved and wanted to be loved. Not the forceful lover he'd come to know as of late, but the man who'd filled Jeff's life with happiness, completed him in ways he'd never expected.

As he lay beneath Mack's warm body, used his tongue to explore every ridge, every vein of Mack's cock, Jeff couldn't help but wish this would last forever. Not only the sex but the intimacy, the union. Just the two of them.

But that had always been his problem, hadn't it? Jeff had never been the sort to settle for temporary. He never did things half-ass, so why should he settle? Only that was exactly what he was doing now because that was all Mack was offering, and God help him, Jeff wanted the man any way he could have him.

Mack shifted, his cock dislodging from Jeff's mouth, and he groaned his displeasure for the move, earning a soft chuckle from Mack.

"Turn over," Mack instructed.

A chill shot down his spine as he rolled onto his stomach. The mattress dipped as Mack moved with him, taking up position between Jeff's legs. Warm hands gripped his hips, pulling them back until he was on his knees, chest flat on the mattress. Jeff closed his eyes, focused on every gentle sweep of Mack's fingers over his skin, the strength in those calloused hands as they massaged his back for a few seconds before drifting lower, cupping his ass, spreading his cheeks.

"You know what I'm gonna do, don't you?" Mack's raspy words teased over his skin.

"Please…"

Mack pressed his lips to Jeff's ass cheek. "You want my tongue, don't you?"

"God, yes." Jeff damn sure wasn't above begging. "Please…"

He was briefly aware of Mack's warm breath over his skin, his firm hands spreading him open wide.

"Oh, fuck," he groaned, his cock jerking when Mack's tongue dipped between his cheeks. "Oh, fuck, Mack."

Mack's rough groan sent vibrations through his body. Jeff rocked his hips, wanting to feel that wicked tongue working him over, sparking those sensitive nerve endings. He managed to slide his hand beneath his body, palming his cock. He stroked in perfect rhythm to Mack's exquisite ministrations. No one but Mack had ever done this to him, ever rimmed him. It had always seemed such a taboo act to Jeff, but when Mack did it, he couldn't even bring himself to care.

Jeff had no idea how much time passed, but Mack continued until Jeff was certain he'd have beard burn between his thighs. Not that he gave a shit, because he couldn't have asked Mack to stop. Not now, not ever. But then he did, but only briefly. Jeff turned his head in the direction of Mack's nightstand, knew what he was reaching for. Every muscle in his body coiled tightly, his cock pulsing in his fist as he waited for Mack's return. He wasn't disappointed, because a minute later, he felt the thick head of Mack's cock sliding across his asshole, then dipping into him, but only a little. Mack worked the head of his cock into Jeff's ass, teasing him ruthlessly before finally giving him more.

Inch by delicious inch, Mack filled him until Jeff was panting, pain morphing with pleasure. Soft moans rattled in his chest when Mack strategically grazed the perfect spot inside him. And once Mack was buried to the hilt, he shifted, his hands pressing into the mattress near Jeff's head as Mack covered him.

"This is what I dream about," Mack said gruffly, pulling his hips back, pushing them forward until they were flat against Jeff's ass.

Jeff closed his eyes, letting the exquisite sound of his words consume him.

"Every night." *Thrust, retreat.* "Being inside you." *In, out.* "So"—*forward*—"deep"—*back ... thrust*—"inside you."

Jeff moaned softly, needing more.

"I never stopped loving you," Mack whispered, his lips brushing Jeff's shoulder as he ground his hips, working his cock as deep as he could go.

Emotion churned within Jeff, intensifying the pleasure, because that was what this was, right? Making love. Not fucking, not satisfying an urge. Mack was loving him the way he used to, with his heart and his body.

Jeff gripped the comforter in one fist, his cock in the other. As Mack rocked into him, he squeezed his flesh, staving off the release that was building. He wanted to spend the rest of the night right here, just like this.

"Tell me you still love me," Mack pleaded, the torment in his words ringing loudly.

"I've always loved you," he answered. "Always will."

That was why he'd come here tonight. Not only for dinner or conversation, not merely for this, but to tell Mack he still loved him, wanted a future with him. The rest of their lives wouldn't be enough, but it would do because he loved the man with every ounce of his being.

"Jeff … oh, fuck, baby."

His insides twisted, heart lurching in his chest as he squeezed his eyes shut and pretended this wasn't going to be the finale for them, but he felt it in the way Mack moved, heard it in the rasp of his voice. The man was torn up inside, fighting battles he would never win because you couldn't control who you loved, and you couldn't be someone you weren't no matter how hard you willed it to be true.

Releasing his cock, Jeff moved his arms, his palms sliding flat so his hands aligned with Mack's. As he'd hoped, Mack shifted, placing his hands atop Jeff's and linking their fingers while Mack took his pleasure from him. Glorious sensations overtook Jeff's body, his mind, as Mack drove deeper inside him, impaling him with long, even strokes. His pace quickened as the seconds ticked by until Mack was grunting, his sweat-slicked chest sliding against Jeff's back.

"Come for me," Jeff urged.

An animalistic growl echoed in the room as Mack's hips shot forward, filling him to the point of pain before retreating and driving in again. Over and over, Mack drove them toward that precarious edge, and Jeff held on, prayed it would last forever. Overwhelming pleasure assaulted him, making his cock pulse and twitch.

Mack warned him only seconds before he exploded, his hands tightening, squeezing Jeff's fingers as he drove in as deep as he could and held himself there. His ass flexed around Mack's cock as his lover came deep inside him. Jeff had expected to feel Mack's weight settle over him, but instead, one thick arm banded around him, pulling Jeff up until he was kneeling, seated on Mack's thick thighs, his ass still impaled.

When Mack fisted his cock, Jeff dropped his head back, resting it on Mack's forehead as that relentless hand jerked him to completion.

"I love you," Mack whispered as Jeff's body drew up tight as a bow when he came.

But despite the fact his body was satiated, his heart and mind were now at war. He couldn't lose this man, and he knew in that instant he would do whatever it took to ensure no one took him away from him.

Not again.

Not ever again.

Chapter Six

Saturday, January 25, 2020

"WE APOLOGIZE FOR COMING ON SUCH SHORT notice," the short redhead said, her smile confident.

Mack realized she didn't appear the least bit remorseful.

"But my clients insisted they see the house today. They've been looking for so long and, as you may know, real estate in Coyote Ridge is quite rare."

Yeah, Mack had heard.

"Anyway, if you wouldn't mind giving us a few minutes to look around…"

When her bright eyes shot to the front door, Mack realized she was dismissing him.

From his own fucking house.

Figured.

While the young couple studied the walls of his kitchen, Mack strolled toward the front door and out onto the porch. He didn't bother grabbing his coat or his boots, stepping out into the chill. How long could they take? A couple of minutes was all that was required to walk all twelve hundred square feet. Twice.

Of course, it was raining and weirdly cold today, so his lack of clothing became apparent quickly. That would be his luck, especially since he had no choice but to hug the wall of the house in an effort to keep what little shelter there was over his head. After five minutes, Mack realized he should've grabbed his boots. Ten minutes and he was wishing he'd grabbed his coat. His gaze shifted to his truck parked in the driveway. Or at the very least, his keys. That way he could've been warm and dry while those strangers invaded his privacy, likely devising a plan to remodel every inch of the house Mack had called home for the past three decades.

He glared at the For Sale sign, wanted to give that stupid smiling picture of Chris the Realtor the finger. Better yet, he wanted to punch that smug bastard in the face. Chris had called him half an hour ago to let him know there were potential buyers coming by and he needed to have the place spic and span and be out as soon as possible. Not much notice, the woman inside had said. Try none.

Irritated at being woken early, Mack hadn't bothered to rush, didn't put his dishes in the dishwasher, nor did he make the effort to make his bed as Chris had suggested. Hell, the bastard was just lucky Mack wasn't still in it. Or Jeff, for that matter. He wasn't sure when the sheriff had slipped out, but he knew it was before dawn. Damn good thing, too.

A good half hour passed as Mack's teeth chattered and his toes went numb, fingers, too, though he'd tucked them beneath his arms in an effort to keep from getting frostbite. Finally the front door opened and the three intruders stepped out. The redheaded Realtor was grinning widely.

"Thank you, Mr. Schwartz, for allowing us to look around. I'll be in touch."

Mack nodded, but rather than hang around to hear her spiel, he slipped back into the house and quickly closed the door, keeping them on the outside.

Instinct had him glancing around, ensuring nothing had been taken. Not that he had anything worth stealing. The old boombox on the side table hadn't worked in at least twelve years. The television was on its last leg, roughly the same age.

Satisfied they hadn't made off with his worthless shit, Mack padded down the hall to his room, fell into the bed, and closed his eyes.

"I KNOW IT'S SATURDAY, AND I HATE to bother you at home, but I thought you'd want to know what I found out."

With his phone to his ear, Travis peered around the living room as his kids argued over who was supposed to be building the block fort they'd been working on for the past hour.

"Give me an hour," he told Reese. "Then I'll meet you at the diner."

"Works for me. See you then."

Travis disconnected the call and tucked his phone in his pocket.

"Who was that?" Gage asked when he appeared from the front hall.

"Reese. Said he's got some info."

Gage spun around when Avery squealed at the top of her lungs, the sound something she'd been perfecting over the past few months.

"I'll take 'em away if you can't behave," Gage warned.

"But, Daddy, it's s'posed to be my turn," Kate argued, holding the block above Avery's head so her younger sister couldn't reach it.

"Share," he ordered, making Travis smile.

Sometimes it was like they were refereeing an MMA fight with these little ones.

"Who wants to go see Grams and Pops?" Travis offered.

Kade bounced to his feet, raising his hand. "I do! I do!"

"I wanna go play with Mason," Kate said, though it hadn't been an option.

"Me, too! Me, too!" Kade shouted, evidently changing his mind at the last second.

Travis sighed and peered over at Gage. "I'll call my mom; you call Kaleb. I'll see if Jess can keep an eye on Haden. If she can, we can drop him by Kylie's office for an hour or so. We'll take Maddox with us to the diner."

"You want me goin' with you?" Gage grinned. "How generous you are to drag me into your schemes."

"As my husband, I figure it's your duty," Travis retorted, then snatched his phone and headed for the kitchen.

An hour later, after they'd dropped Kade and Kate off with Zoey, Travis had made a pit stop at his parents', where they delivered Avery for the afternoon, then over to Kylie's office so Jess could keep an eye on Haden. Of course, they were ten minutes late getting to the diner, but that was par for the course when you had five kids to tote around town.

"Hey, little guy," Reese greeted Maddox.

Feeling generous, Travis passed the eight-month-old over before joining Gage in the booth opposite Reese.

The waitress came over, delivered a highchair, then smiled widely as she stared down at Reese and Maddox.

"Oh, he's gettin' so big," she said with a wide grin.

"Wonder how often Reese hears that?" Gage whispered in Travis's ear, making him laugh.

Reese looked up, narrowed his eyes in warning, which only made Travis laugh again.

"What can I get you boys?" she asked after she'd cooed over Maddox. Or Reese. He wasn't quite sure who she was enamored with more.

"Two sweet teas," Gage told her. "No food for us."

She nodded, then sauntered off, Reese's gaze following her.

"What'd you find out?" Travis asked, getting right to the point.

"A lot of things, actually," Reese said as he put Maddox into the highchair.

Gage passed over a couple of cookies he'd retrieved from Maddox's go-bag.

"But it was what I didn't find out that was the most revealing," Reese explained.

"Such as?"

"Well, I did as you requested, looked into his personal life. I had my brother dig up the dirt on his financials. Nothing out of the ordinary there. Guy hordes money like it's going out of style."

"Tell Z I appreciate his help," Travis told him, referring to Reese's older brother Zachariah, known affectionately by his friends and family as simply Z.

"Already did." Reese paused while the waitress delivered two iced teas and a grilled chicken salad Reese had evidently ordered before their arrival.

"Watchin' the figure?" Gage teased, nodding at the overflow of greens in front of Reese.

"Always." Reese picked up his fork, stabbed some lettuce, then peered up at Travis. "Anyway. The most interesting thing I learned is that Daniel is dating a woman named Phoebe Monroe."

Travis squeezed his lemon into his tea, dropped the wedge into the glass. "Why's that interesting?"

"Well, Phoebe Monroe has quite the social life. Girl's always out and about, all over Austin. I get the feelin' she's quite into the Sixth Street scene based on her social media."

Travis wasn't sure where Reese was going with this, but he refrained from grilling him, hoping the man would get to the point soon.

"And she's tethered to her Instagram account. Posts at least two dozen pictures every single day." Reese took a bite, chewed, reached for his ice water, drank. Very efficient in his movements. "Odd thing is, her boyfriend of four years isn't in any of those pictures."

"Maybe Daniel's camera shy," Gage noted.

Reese took another bite, shook his head. "Oh, no. Definitely not the case. His Instagram's overflowing, too."

Travis peered at Gage, over to Maddox, back to Reese. "And what does this mean to me?"

"Daniel and Phoebe have been together for four years, even have it noted on their Facebook relationship statuses, but Daniel's only been in one picture with her in all that time. Just so happens to be a picture of roughly half a dozen people." Reese washed down another bite with water. "Only ol' Danny-boy's not snugglin' up to the blond princess."

Travis frowned, waiting not-so-patiently for the point.

Reese held up his fork, like a light bulb over his head. He held it there while he grabbed his phone, brought the screen to life with one hand, then set it on the table and slid it over to Travis.

"That's the picture."

"Well, I'll be damned," Travis grumbled.

Gage bumped his shoulder. "Looks like you really were onto something."

———

JEFF PULLED INTO THE PARKING LOT OF the diner and maneuvered into a spot beside Kennedy's. He hopped out and instantly smiled at the two faces beaming up at him from the back seat of Kennedy's SUV. When he heard the locks disengage, he opened the door and leaned inside.

"What's goin' on, little guys?" he asked his grandsons, who were now smiling ear to ear.

"We have dinner with Pawpaw," Matthew said in his three-year-old speak.

"Yes, you are havin' dinner with Pawpaw," he told him as he unbuckled Brody from his car seat and hefted the eighteen-month-old into his arms. "I think you've gained weight, little man."

Brody tugged at his hair and planted a sloppy wet kiss on Jeff's cheek, making him chuckle.

Kennedy opened the opposite door, released Matthew's fancy-ride buckles. But rather than take her hand, the little guy crawled over Brody's seat and popped out of the car on Jeff's side. He took Jeff's hand and proceeded to lead the way into the restaurant, hungry based on his urgent tug on his hand.

With both his hands occupied, he was unable to open the door for his daughter, but once she swung it wide, Jeff held it with his foot, allowing her to walk inside.

Once they were at the table—Brody in a highchair, Matthew standing in the booth beside him, and Kennedy across from him—Jeff turned his attention to Kennedy.

"Not that I mind havin' dinner with my daughter," he said, "but is everything all right?"

She smiled brightly. "Yes. Absolutely. It's just been too long, and I knew if I didn't make time, it wouldn't make itself."

Jeff exhaled slowly, relaxed for the first time since he'd gotten her call that morning. As much as he pretended to be an optimist, these days Jeff spent more time waiting for the other shoe to drop. And while he knew Kennedy was blissfully happy with Sawyer, he still worried about his only child.

Kennedy leaned forward. "Did you really think something was wrong?"

He forced a smile. "No. But a dad has a right to worry, right?"

She smiled, the move reaching her pretty hazel eyes that looked so much like his, most people didn't realize she was adopted. Not that he shared that news with many people. As far as he was concerned, Kennedy was his flesh and blood, his most prized accomplishment in life.

"You look tired," he told her. Not that he was surprised to see dark circles under her eyes. His daughter worked too hard, and what time she didn't spend at the veterinary clinic, she was making up for her time away with her kids and Sawyer. Sometimes he wondered if she ever sat still.

"Yeah, well, I'm getting used to it. So, how's work?" she asked, opening her menu.

Matthew took Jeff's menu and mimicked his mother's movements, staring down at it intently as though he could make out the words.

He pointed to a picture. "I want that, Pawpaw."

"I'm not so sure you'll like liver and onions," he told the boy. "How about chicken nuggets?"

As though he'd just lassoed the moon and dragged it down from the sky, Matthew threw his arms around Jeff's neck. "Yes! Chicken nuggets. That's the best idea!"

Jeff laughed, peered over at Brody. "And what about you, little man?"

The little boy nodded excitedly.

"Chicken nuggets it is."

It took a few minutes, but they managed to order drinks and dinner, then settled the boys with packages of saltines while they waited.

"Back to my original question," Kennedy said with a chuckle. "How's work?"

"Same ol', same ol'. It's been quiet, actually."

"You say that like it's a bad thing."

"Figure it's the calm before the storm." He was used to certain incidents in Coyote Ridge—neighbors bickering, minor infractions such as shoplifting, complaints about the disrepair of the roads—and when things got too quiet, it usually meant something big was coming.

"Did you see the sign in front of Moonshiners?" Kennedy asked, keeping her voice low.

Jeff leaned back when Matthew reached over him to pass Brody another cracker.

"Yeah," he said, hoping he didn't sound as disappointed as he felt.

"When Sawyer told me Mack was selling, I thought it was a joke. Then I saw the sign."

Jeff hadn't thought it was a joke, but he'd honestly been hoping Mack would change his mind.

"Have you talked to him?" she asked.

"Not about the bar, no." That much was true.

Kennedy studied him for a moment, and he knew his daughter saw more than most people did. Then again, Jeff didn't try to hide anything from her. While he'd never come out and told her he was gay, he hadn't lied about it when she'd confronted him. When she was growing up, he'd focused solely on being the best father he could be, and that had left little time for relationships, so it never was an issue. From the moment her adoption went through, Jeff had found his way, the path he was meant to be on. Raising her had been the highlight of his life, and watching her now, seeing the intelligent, beautiful woman she'd turned into made him proud whether he deserved any credit or not.

"I find it hard to believe he wants to up and leave Coyote Ridge," she said, her eyes intently focused on his face as though reading every line.

"Yeah, well."

"Dad, his son's making him do this."

"No one makes Mack do anything," he assured her. "It's his choice."

"Have you told him how you feel?" Her voice was lower than before.

Jeff wiped the condensation off his tea glass, unable to look her in the eye. "I have, yeah."

"Lately?"

He lifted his gaze, met her concerned stare. "Yes. It's not enough," he admitted, the words widening the hole in his chest.

Kennedy's hand covered his. "I thought for sure you two would work things out. You were happy together once."

Yes, they were.

"I can't believe you're not fighting for him."

Mack

Oh, he'd been fighting, all right. But with every failed battle, he was losing hope that he could win the war.

"I'm so sorry, Dad."

Matthew stood, threw his arms around Jeff's neck. "Me, too, Pawpaw. So sorry."

He couldn't help it, he smiled, patting Matthew's arm, though deep down, his heart was breaking just a little more.

Chapter Seven

Sunday, January 26, 2020

THOUGH MACK GENERALLY WORKED SEVEN DAYS A week, he'd been taking Sundays off as of late. With Rafe willing to fill in at the bar, it had worked out.

It should've been a reprieve, a chance to sit back, unwind, breathe easier, but Mack generally found himself wired for sound. Tonight was no exception. Unable to relax, he was pacing the small, square living room, the tiny, elongated kitchen, anything to keep from picking up the stack of papers he'd been delivered during last night's shift. He'd managed to wait until closing before he opened them, and at that point, he had wished he hadn't bothered.

Pausing in his pursuit to flatten all the spots in the floor, he stared down at the cover letter. His gaze slid from the logo in the top corner, past his name and address, down to the subject line: OFFER TO PURCHASE MOONSHINERS.

He wished Jeff was there so he could talk to someone about this. As it was, he had no one. Daniel had made sure of that, his disapproval the guiding light for his every move. While this news would've likely put his son over the moon, Mack couldn't bring himself to call his son. Not yet. Not until he'd come to terms with it.

Of course, he knew that was never going to happen.

Mack resumed pacing, his gaze shifting to the clock on the wall. One twenty-three p.m. Church was officially out, and most of the parishioners were likely back in their homes, settling down to their Sunday lunch as they did every week. The diner would be crowded because the people of Coyote Ridge loved to congregate in public, and though Mack had never been one of those people, he realized it settled him to know that it was still taking place around him. In the small town he'd grown up in, spent his life in. The town he couldn't imagine moving away from.

His cell phone rang, the vibration making it buzz on the Formica countertop. With a resigned sigh, he glanced down at it, frowned.

He considered letting it go to voicemail but caved before it could.

"Hello," he greeted the caller.

"Michael? It's Chris."

There was a smile in the Realtor's voice.

"I'm calling with some good news. We got an offer on your house, and I'm happy to say it's far better than I was expecting. I was wondering if it would be possible to meet with you. I'd like to go over it with you face-to-face. Would three o'clock work?"

"No," he said abruptly, then took a deep breath. "Sorry, I've got an errand to run this afternoon. But you can come by the bar tomorrow night."

"Uh … all right. I guess I'll see you tomorrow then. Let's make it six o'clock."

"I'll be there," he assured Chris, then disconnected.

With his phone still in his hand, Mack grabbed the stack of papers, along with his wallet and his keys, then stormed out of the house, not bothering to grab a coat or lock the door behind him.

A few minutes later, he was pulling along the curb in front of Jeff's sprawling 1970s ranch house. It looked the same as it always had with its wide front porch outlined in white trim. The style was different than the fancy Victorian Jeff had once fancied, and truth be told, Mack much preferred this. Each end of the house matched the other, though one was a side-facing garage, the other three bedrooms and two large bathrooms. Mack thought about all the nights he'd spent here, the conversations he and Jeff had shared regarding Mack moving in with him. That had never happened, which was only one of the many regrets Mack had.

Jeff's police-issue cruiser was parked in the driveway, and Mack knew the old Ford truck he loved was in the garage because Jeff didn't take it out much anymore.

Figuring it was only a matter of time before Jeff realized he was parked outside, Mack forced his weary body out of the truck. He grabbed the stack of papers, held them against his chest as he marched over the brittle grass that would soon return to its glorious green once spring made its way back around.

His boots sounded loud on the wooden porch, his knuckles louder on the door. Mack didn't bother stepping back. For one, he didn't have the energy, and two, if he did, he feared he would simply turn around and run.

"Mack?" Jeff greeted when he pulled the glossy blue door open, his salt-and-pepper eyebrows lowering as though he was both surprised and concerned to find Mack there.

Rather than speak, he shoved the papers in Jeff's direction.

"Come in," Jeff said, relieving him of the documents before stepping backward. "Why are you not wearin' a coat?"

Mack shrugged, glad to see his legs still worked as he walked into the wide-open space. He'd loved this house, but not because of its country charm. More so because it felt like a home, unlike the three bedrooms he occupied only a few blocks over. Jeff's house was bright and airy, a hint of cinnamon drifting from one of the candles he had always kept burning in the kitchen.

The door closed behind him, and Mack was aware of Jeff's footsteps following him deeper into the house.

"I just made a pot of coffee," Jeff told him. "Would you like some?"

Mack nodded, continued toward the kitchen.

Jeff set the papers on the small pedestal table with its matching white, spindle-backed chairs. The blinds covering the windows in the breakfast nook were all open, letting in the brilliant winter light. The backyard looked the same as always, with the exception of the blue and white doghouse that used to sit unoccupied in the grass. Jeff's golden retriever—Teddy—had passed away a few years ago, and it looked as though Jeff had opted not to get another four-legged companion. He briefly wondered if he would one day.

"Thanks," Mack said when Jeff handed him a white cup.

"Sit," Jeff urged, nodding to one of the chairs.

He did.

Jeff joined him, pulling the stack of papers toward him. "This looks like an offer for the bar."

"It is."

Mack remained quiet while Jeff skimmed the pages.

"It looks like a good offer to me," Jeff finally said, his tone uneasy, as though he didn't know what Mack expected him to say.

"Travis seems rather intent on acquirin' it," Mack snapped, the heat of his words fizzling out before he finished the sentence.

Jeff set his mug down and turned his attention to him. "I don't think that's what this is."

"No?" Mack nodded toward the papers. "Quite a bit over the asking price. Seems pretty insistent to me."

Jeff sighed, then reached over and touched his arm. "Mack, I think you're missing the point here."

Mack stared down at the hand on his arm. "And what might that be?"

"Travis is ensuring you don't sell it to anyone else. His offer reflects his desire to be the highest, just in case."

Lifting his gaze, he locked eyes with Jeff. "Just in case what?"

For the first time since they'd renewed whatever this was, Mack saw true pain in Jeff's eyes when he said, "In case you really go through with this."

Mack swallowed hard, his throat clogged with emotion. He'd tried to battle it back since he'd read the words on the cover letter for the first time, but they were closing in on him now.

Though the emotion tore at his voice, he finally said aloud what he'd been thinking all along, "I don't want to sell, Jeff." He inhaled deeply, forcing down a sob. "I don't want to sell."

WITH HIS HAND STILL ON MACK'S ARM, Jeff offered a comforting squeeze.

"I don't want to leave," Mack rasped, the words coming out as though they'd been held in for too long.

It was rare for Mack to show so much emotion. Sure, they could connect on an intimate level, but Jeff couldn't remember the last time Mack had opened up about personal things. He'd always been the kind to bottle it up, pretend it didn't exist, even when their relationship had been growing strong. It had always required chipping away at the hard exterior before revealing anything soft inside the handsome man.

"Then don't leave."

"I have to." Mack pulled his hand back. "I owe it to my son."

Jeff felt that familiar anger rushing to the surface. "The only thing you owe that boy is your unconditional love. But he owes you that, too, Mack."

Mack's blue eyes reflected the torment inside him. "I lied to him. This is how I can make it up to him."

Jeff laughed without mirth. "Is it? And what happens when you sell everything you own? When you uproot your life and relocate to be closer to him. How does that benefit him?"

"He'll know I'm doing what he's asked of me."

Shaking his head, Jeff pushed to his feet. "And what? You become someone you're not? Or no, wait. You *pretend* to be someone you're not? Because we both know it doesn't matter where you live. You'll still be gay, Mack. You'll just be an unhappy gay man who lives out the rest of his life alone."

Mack didn't look up.

"Have you ever asked yourself why it's so important to Daniel that you become someone else?"

"It doesn't matter."

"Oh, it fucking matters."

Mack's eyes flew up, likely surprised by the curse. Jeff tended to keep his language on the PG level most of the time. One of the by-products of being in the public eye.

"I've wondered on numerous occasions what his end game is," Jeff admitted. "I've sat back for the past four years and watched as he tugged and pulled at the threads of your life, using those strings to position you how he wants you. Somewhere along the way, you seem to have forgotten that you raised that boy. You did everything in your power to make him happy. And your sexual orientation is none of his goddamn business, Mack."

"I left his mother because I was gay," Mack blurted. "It's damn sure his business."

Jeff barked a laugh. "No. That was your business. And hers. Not his. He doesn't get to dictate how things play out because he got his feelings hurt when he learned your secret. You being gay didn't make you a bad father. Sure, it made you a shitty husband to a woman, but lessons learned, right? We all make mistakes, and we learn from them. We don't turn our lives upside down to atone for them because someone's feelings were hurt. And in this case, I doubt it was Daniel's."

Jeff continued to pace, hands clenching at his sides as all the words he'd wanted to say to Mack over the years came barreling out.

"We were happy, Mack. Fucking happy. Right up until your son decided you shouldn't be. He decided you couldn't be gay because it gave him power over you. And fine. I'll admit you broke my goddamn heart when you turned your back on me, but I didn't attempt to restructure your life because of it. No. I sat back and waited, loving you from a distance because I knew deep down I would never love anyone else the way I love you."

Mack was watching him now. Jeff could feel his eyes following him and he wondered if Mack heard his use of present tense. He still loved him. That would never change.

"And you did what Daniel wanted," Jeff continued. "You ended things. You didn't date, and I assume that's because you're not interested in women. You can pretend to be straight, but it's somethin' else entirely to go through the motions. He won that round.

"But how does selling the bar and your house, moving to Austin, and being referred to as Michael do anyone any good? Do you really think Daniel'll be happy with that? He won't. Next thing you know, he'll be picking out your clothes, decorating your house. Why? Why does he want to do that?" Jeff turned to look at Mack. "He's compensating for something. Ever wonder what that is? Why he's pushin' you so fucking hard?"

Still no response, but Jeff knew the man was paying attention, so he kept going.

"You want to sell your house? Sell it. You don't live there, anyway. You sleep there. It's a box with windows and a door that you use for shelter. You want to move? Move." Jeff swung his arm around. "Move in here. It's where you belong. Here. With me. You might try to contradict me, but I know you'd be happy here. We both would because we were happy, Mack. We were fucking happy before you left me." Emotion contorted his words, but he plowed forward. "I love you, Mack. I've always loved you and I always will. This thing"—Jeff motioned between them—"it's not about sex. It's about connecting with you because I fucking love you. I want you back. There. I said it. I don't want you to move." His breath hitched. "I don't want to lose you again."

Mack finally moved but Jeff stood where he was, staring at him, waiting for the repercussions of his words.

"Every word I said is the truth," he continued. "I will not take them back. I will not regret telling you how I feel, because it has been eating me up inside. If you want to turn me away again, Mack, fine. I'll deal with it, but I can't keep going on without you knowing how I feel, without knowing that I—"

Mack cupped his face, stared back at him with so much emotion churning in his eyes it robbed Jeff of his thoughts.

"I love you, Mack," he whispered, willing him to hear the sincerity.

"I love you, too. Never stopped." Mack stepped closer. "And I never meant to hurt you."

"But you did. Watching you walk away tore me up inside. I don't want to do that again."

"I know." Mack leaned forward, kissed him softly. "And I'm sorry."

Jeff pulled back, stared at him. "Don't apologize. Just make it right."

Mack was silent for the longest time before he finally nodded. "Okay."

"Okay, what?"

"I'll make it right."

Jeff's mind whirled, hope blooming deep down. "What does that mean?"

"I—"

A knock on the door caused Mack to stop. Jeff wanted to grab his shotgun and aim it at the door, because damn it, whoever it was had the worst damn timing.

Chapter Eight

MACK WENT INTO THE KITCHEN WHILE JEFF answered the door. He needed a moment to rein himself in because the conversation he'd come here for had taken a turn that both shocked and soothed him. He wanted Jeff to get rid of the visitor so they could continue, to finally clear the air between them.

"Is Mack here?"

Frowning at the familiar voice, Mack stepped out of the kitchen and into the living room. He had a direct line of sight to the front door, where Travis Walker stood, his husband just a few feet behind him.

"I saw your truck," Travis said, evidently explaining why he was there. "Could we talk?"

"Mack hasn't had a chance to look over your offer," Jeff told him.

Travis's eyes remained locked on Mack. "It's not about the offer."

Jeff peered back over his shoulder, as though seeking Mack's approval. Mack nodded.

"Come in."

Travis did, moving toward Mack with a grace that most men his size didn't have. Although he was wearing black slacks and a white button-down—likely what he'd worn to church—he looked as at home in that attire as he did when he was sporting boots and jeans.

"Can I get you some coffee?" Jeff offered.

Mack continued to stare at Travis, wondering if the man even knew how shitty his timing was.

"That would be great," Gage answered.

Mack cast a quick look at Jeff before turning his attention back to Travis. "What did you want to talk about?"

"May we sit?" Travis motioned toward the small table.

He answered by walking over and taking the chair he'd vacated earlier. Travis joined him, and a minute later, Gage and Jeff did, passing out coffee.

"I'm gonna preface this with an apology," Travis said, his voice calm.

Mack frowned.

"You'll understand why in a minute," Gage muttered.

Travis cut his eyes to Gage, blinked slowly, then pinned those steel-blue eyes back on Mack.

"You've known me my entire life, Mack. And I'm sure you're well aware that I have a tendency to overstep."

That was an understatement, but Mack didn't reply, simply lifted a brow, urging Travis to continue.

"In my defense, I only do so when it comes to family. And while there's no blood relation, I've always considered you family."

Mack picked up his coffee, took a sip. More as a distraction than out of need.

"When I first learned you were gonna sell the bar, I was pissed. Not because I want the damn thing, either. Honestly, I don't need the fucking hassle." Travis clasped his hands together on the table, leaned forward. "I was pissed because I knew you didn't want to sell it. Yeah, I staged that whole incident last week. Because I wanted to show you we have your back. I went to stand up for you if you needed me to. Of course, my best intentions are generally not thought out completely."

Travis's gaze swung to the papers sitting in the middle of the table.

"The offer was a way of showing you the same. I don't want to buy the bar, but I will if I have to, because it's your bar, Mack. And if you choose to leave, I can't very well stop you, but I can damn sure make certain your family's business continues as it always has. The folks in this town, we go there as much to drink as we do to be in your company." He smirked. "Not that you're the best company considerin' your lack of conversation, but that's not the point. Like I said, you're family and Moonshiners wouldn't be the same without you."

Mack let the words sink in, but he didn't know what to say.

"But that's not why I'm here. I came to let you in on a little secret. A secret I unearthed recently. Yes, I know I stick my nose in when I shouldn't because my husband and wife tell me that all the damn time. Doesn't mean I'll change, doesn't even mean I want to. I wanted to give you the information and you can do with it as you will. It won't leave this room, and I can assure you, I won't say a word to Daniel."

Mack frowned. "Daniel? What are you talkin' about?"

Travis seemed to consider his words carefully before speaking. "I had someone look into Daniel's background."

"You had no right to do that," Mack snarled.

Travis sat up straight. "No, I didn't. Doesn't change things." He retrieved his phone from his pocket, set it on the table. "I've wondered for a long time why Daniel's been so insistent to turn you into Michael Schwartz, the straight man who lives in Austin, under his thumb. It wasn't until he brought that Chris guy to town to talk to you that I got suspicious. There was something off about that incident."

There was a lot off about it, but again, Mack remained quiet.

"I noticed something about Daniel's body language that day. Specifically regarding his interaction with Chris."

Mack glanced at Jeff, noticed the man was hanging on every word.

"And when I'm curious, I tend to react. So, I did some digging. Did you know Daniel's been dating a woman named Phoebe?"

Mack nodded. "I knew there was a woman. Didn't know her name, but they've been on and off for several years."

Travis held his stare for a minute. "No, they've been pretending to date for four years. Back around the time Daniel insisted you go straight."

Gage chuckled, clearly amused by the turn of phrase.

"Phoebe and Daniel never dated," Travis continued. "They've never been a couple at all. Phoebe is Chris's half-sister. Different mothers, but they grew up together."

Mack wasn't sure where this was going.

Travis glanced at Jeff, then back to him. "Daniel's been with Chris all along."

Mack sat up, eyebrows shooting toward his hairline. "What?"

"Mack, Daniel's gay."

Shaking his head, he started to push his chair back. "That's bullshit. I don't know what you're tryin' to—"

Travis pushed his phone across the table.

There was a picture of Daniel and Chris on the screen. They were standing with several others, and while Chris had his arm around Daniel's shoulders, that didn't mean a thing.

Travis reached over, swiped across the screen, and another image appeared. This one showing Chris and Daniel in a lip-lock.

Another swipe, another picture.

Chris and Daniel staring at one another, the unmistakable look of love on both their faces.

Mack glanced at Jeff. "I don't understand."

"I don't know his reasons for hidin' who he is or pretendin' to be someone he's not," Travis said, "but I get the feelin' he's ashamed."

"Why would he be? He knows I'm gay. Who does he have to hide from?"

Gage was the one to answer. "Probably from his mother."

Well, hell.

Jeff's brain was going a million miles a minute, rehashing everything Travis had told them. Even half an hour after Travis and Gage left, he was still speechless, unable to come up with a single thing that might ease the tension he could feel pouring off Mack.

As he sat on the couch, he watched the big guy pace back and forth across the ivory rug, bumping the wooden coffee table every so often by accident.

"So what did he think he would do? Make my life hell because he has to hide from his mother?" Mack looked up briefly. "Does he think it's my fault he's gay? Maybe he's punishing me for it?"

They both knew it wasn't hereditary, so Jeff kept his mouth shut, figuring it was best to let Mack talk this one out.

"How does making me move help this situation? Making me sell the bar?"

Jeff tracked him with his eyes. "The only sure way to find the answers is to talk to Daniel."

Mack stopped, put his hands on his hips, and pinned Jeff with a stare. "And how do I broach that subject? Hey, Daniel, word is you're gay. That true? Welcome to the club, son." Mack shook his head, started moving again. "I don't see how that's gonna win me any points with him."

"Maybe not, but it does help to make some sense out of all this. We both know Meredith loved you when you were with her. And she hated you when she learned you couldn't love her back. She promised to keep your secret, but then she confirmed Daniel's suspicions. Because of her past feelings for you, I'm sure that conversation didn't go over well."

"I don't think she's homophobic," Mack said.

"I don't, either. I think she was a jilted lover and there was no way for her to fix you, because you weren't broken. You simply couldn't give her what she needed. I'm sure she shouted her hatred to the rooftops, used your sexuality against you. Daniel likely believes she'll hate him, too, if she finds out."

Mack's head popped up. "She could never hate him. Meredith loves him. She was a good mom even if she did hate me."

"You know that," Jeff said, "but Daniel is likely too confused to realize it. Or maybe he's just scared. Lashing out at you because of it. People do stupid things when they're scared."

When Mack finally dropped onto the couch beside him, Jeff shifted so he could face him more fully. Mack was holding his cell phone in his hand. Every now and then, he would bring the screen to life only to darken it once more. He sat patiently, wondering if Mack would give in and call Daniel.

When he finally set the phone on the table, Jeff reverted back to the conversation they'd been having before Travis showed up.

"Earlier, when you said you would make things right ... what did you mean?"

Mack looked over at him, his expression going blank for a moment.

"Before Travis dropped that anvil on your head."

Mack smiled and let his head dip forward as though he was shy.

"Mack?"

"Chris is comin' by the bar tomorrow night."

Confused as to what the hell Mack was talking about, Jeff waited him out.

Mack cut a sideways glance his way. "He got an offer on my house."

Jeff stared, still unsure where this was going.

"I'm gonna accept the offer," Mack stated.

Swallowing hard, he nodded. "Is it a good one?"

Mack turned, his knee bumping Jeff's. "I have no idea, but I don't care."

"So you're going through with it? You're gonna move to Austin? Even after you learned about—"

Mack's hand came up to cover Jeff's mouth, effectively cutting him off.

Jeff's eyes widened when Mack scooted closer.

"Did you mean what you said earlier?" Mack asked, lowering his hand.

"I said a lot of things," Jeff countered, trying to filter through their conversation.

"About me moving in here."

His breath halted in his lungs even as he nodded.

Mack shifted closer, cupped his face. "I want to be with you, Jeff. It's the only thing I've ever wanted."

More nodding, no words forming because his throat was closing from an overload of emotion.

"I'll accept the offer on the house because you're right. It's not home. Never has been."

"And the bar?" Jeff forced past the lump in his throat.

"I'm not sellin' Moonshiners. I don't want to leave Coyote Ridge. I don't want to leave you. So for as long as you'll have me … this is where I want to be."

Again with the nod, but this time Jeff reached for Mack, pulling him closer, their lips meeting. Mack took over from there, easing over Jeff as they laid out on the couch, chest to chest.

"I've got a lot to make up for," Mack whispered, staring down at him.

"No you don't."

"I do. And I'll spend the rest of my life making it up to you. I'll make sure not a day passes that you don't know how much I love you."

Jeff already knew, even during the years when Mack had pretended otherwise. Sure, they'd kept their distance, but the fact that neither one of them had moved on was proof that it was only a matter of time. Would he change anything? Damn right he would. He would've never let Mack walk out on him that day if he'd known he would spend years without him. But since he couldn't modify the past, he would adjust the future.

And this time he would make sure Mack couldn't walk away. Not without a legal battle, anyway.

Jeff pushed at Mack's chest. "Get up. I want to show you something."

With uncertainty glittering in his eyes, Mack did as he instructed. When Jeff got to his feet, he took Mack's hand, led him down the hallway to the master bedroom.

"I like where your head's at, sheriff," Mack said when Jeff pressed up against his back.

"Notice anything?"

Mack glanced back over his shoulder. "I notice you're not naked yet."

"Not yet," he agreed. "Anything else?"

Mack shrugged, then turned back to the room. Jeff felt his body tighten and he knew what he saw.

"Those are my reading glasses."

"Yes."

"And my alarm clock."

"Mmm-hmm."

Mack's voice lowered an octave. "And the book I was reading the night before…"

"The night before you left," Jeff whispered against his ear. "I've never moved any of it."

When Mack turned, Jeff cupped his face.

"Like I said, I love you, Mack."

A rough growl escaped the big man, and a few minutes later, they were both naked.

Chapter Nine

Monday, January 27, 2020

MACK WAS FINISHING UP HIS OPENING CHECKLIST when Chris arrived, walking into the bar, his gaze quickly scanning as though he expected to find a monster lurking.

"Chris," Mack greeted.

"I didn't realize you weren't open yet."

"Yeah, well, it's not a twenty-four-hour joint."

"I should've done my research, Michael, I apologize."

"Mack," he corrected the young man. "Not Michael. Only one person calls me Michael and I intend to keep it that way."

Chris's brown eyes settled over him, wide and bright, clearly surprised by the assertive response. "I apologize."

"Sounds to me like you do a little too much of that," Mack noted as he put the last wineglass in place. "Can I get you somethin'? Seltzer water? Beer?"

Once again, Chris scanned the room.

"Are you expectin' someone?"

"Well, I … I thought Daniel was meeting me."

"Ah." Mack nodded. "Are we seeking his approval for the offer?"

Chris's gaze slammed into his. "No. Of course not."

"Good." Mack nodded to the papers in Chris's hand. "Then shall we get started? I do open in an hour."

Chris managed to get his things laid out on the bar, but based on the way his hands were trembling, his anxiety level continued to rise.

"I'm happy to say we received a very encouraging offer," Chris began.

"Skip the spiel, kid. I'm acceptin' the offer."

Those confused eyes landed on Mack once more. "I'm not sure I understand. You don't even know what it is."

"It doesn't matter. I set out to sell the house, you got me an offer, and I have to assume you've got my best interest in mind because of your relationship with my son." Mack wiped the bar top, purposely looking away from the man.

"I'm sorry." Chris cleared his throat. "Relationship?"

Mack looked up, raised his eyebrows. "You're friends, are you not?"

"Friends." Relief swept across his face. "Yes, of course. We're friends."

"Then I doubt you'd do anything to undermine me, right?"

"No, absolutely not."

"Good, then I'll take the offer."

Chris swallowed again, then nodded, closing the manila folder. "Well, then, I can get the paperwork together, but I do suggest you review the offer before signing it. Just in case anything stands out."

"I will."

"Should we talk about the other property?"

Mack stood tall, wiped his hands on a dry towel. "Other property?"

Those wary brown eyes darted around the space once more. "I really thought Daniel would be here for this part."

As though he was summoned, the front door opened and in walked Daniel. He seemed as surprised as Chris to see the place empty.

"Father, it's good to see you."

Mack didn't miss the way Daniel's hand casually slid over Chris's shoulder as he passed by. The kid probably didn't even realize he did it, something he was used to doing to reassure Chris he was there. Jeff used to do the same to Mack all the time.

How the hell had he not figured it out before? Surely the signs had been there, hadn't they? Or was Daniel merely that good at hiding?

"Your father's decided to accept the offer on the house," Chris told him, his voice wavering slightly.

Daniel's eyes widened briefly. "Really? That's … uh … that's fantastic."

Mack dropped the dish towel and put his hands on his hips. "Is it? You don't sound all that thrilled, and here I was thinkin' this was your idea."

The door opened once more. This time Jeff sauntered in wearing his sheriff getup. He offered a wave, then moved behind the bar. "Mind if I grab a Coke?"

"What's mine is yours," Mack said, feeling those little bands on his heart loosen a little more.

Jeff grabbed a cold can from the fridge under the bar, then stood tall. He looked at Chris and smiled. "You must be Chris. The Realtor. I hear you got an offer on Mack's house."

With subtle reluctance, Chris extended his arm to shake Jeff's proffered hand.

"Yes, I am. And yes, I did. We were just talking about it."

"They seem a bit confused that I'd accept the offer," Mack explained, glancing between Daniel and Chris. "I'm tryin' to figure out the punch line."

"It's a good thing, right?" Jeff prompted, his full attention on Daniel.

"Of course it is," Daniel said. "Now we ... I mean, *Chris*, just needs to draw up the paperwork."

"Which," Chris said, "I guess, we should ... I mean, *I* should probably do soon."

Yep, they were definitely a couple. Had been for a long time, because the "we" had become instinctual.

As though eager to get out of the bar, Chris got to his feet. "I'll just go do that now."

"No need to rush off," Mack told him. "Why don't you stay. Have a beer. We can celebrate."

Chris's gaze darted to Daniel as though the man would help him out.

"Is there a problem?" Mack asked, not moving away when Jeff stepped closer. "Somethin' you're not tellin' me?"

Daniel cleared his throat. "Why would you ask that?"

Jeff was the one to answer. "Well, for starters, there's a lot of 'I mean' and questions answering questions. I've been at this game a long time, and I can sense when someone's holdin' somethin' back."

A long exhale escaped Daniel as he stared at the floor and shuffled his feet. When he finally looked up, he met Mack's eyes for the first time since he walked into the bar.

"I just thought you'd put up more of a fight, that's all. I guess ... well, I thought..."

Then it hit Mack what was really going on here. He frowned and was doubly grateful Jeff was nearby.

"A fight? You were lookin' for ... for what, Daniel?" he asked his son. "For me to refuse to sell my house? Or my bar? Or both?"

Daniel didn't answer, but the sheepish look on his face answered for him.

"You *wanted* me to turn you down," Mack said roughly.

Daniel's blue eyes blazed with anger. "Yes, fine! I did." He exhaled on a huff. "I thought you had more backbone than this, Dad."

Ah, so he was back to being Dad and not Father. Good to know.

"I saw how easy it was for you to ... to stop being gay and... Fuck."

Mack barked a laugh, reached up and touched Jeff's hand when it rested on his shoulder. "Stop bein' gay, huh? So you think that's really a thing?"

"Isn't it?" Daniel snapped, but his eyes dropped to Mack's hand covering Jeff's. "You lied to me," he accused.

"No, I didn't. I did as you requested. I broke things off with Jeff when you insisted I do so." Mack's anger deepened his voice. "I've spent the past four years aching for the only real love I've ever known. Because you demanded it, because you said I owed you."

Daniel's eyes widened, his expression one of horror.

And suddenly, it all made perfect fucking sense.

"Is *that* when I failed you?" he asked. "You didn't expect me to go through with it, did you?"

Daniel's lips clamped together.

"That was the wrong response, wasn't it?"

How the hell had he been so blind?

When Daniel didn't respond, Mack continued. "So, what? You decided on a different tack? You were pushin' me, tryin' to get me to break." Mack cursed under his breath. "All because you can't find your way out of the goddamn closet."

Chris inhaled sharply as he backed toward the door.

"You," Jeff said, pointing at him. "Stay. You'll wanna hear this."

To Mack's surprise, Daniel didn't have a comeback. His Adam's apple bobbed up and down, his eyes bouncing over Mack's face.

"Why'd you do it?" Mack demanded.

"You didn't defend yourself, Dad. I thought you would tell me to go to hell, that you loved him. But you didn't. You walked away from him because I told you to."

"I did." Mack couldn't deny it. He wouldn't. "You're my son. I've been riddled with guilt for most of your life, kid. I'd walk through fire to make up for my wrongs where you're concerned."

"You acted like it was no big deal, like it was easy to turn away from him." Daniel glared at Mack. "And that pissed me off most because I lived with my mother telling me how only an abomination could love someone of the same sex. She did keep your secret, but only because I was too young to realize she was always talking about you. I thought she was just a bigot. And when I confronted her, she told me in explicit detail how you're going to hell for your choices. What was I supposed to do? I had no choice but to agree with her. The things she says ... it's disgusting and not only because my father's gay."

"Because you are, too," Mack said softly, swallowing the emotion.

Daniel laughed, a tormented sound. "Yeah. Imagine what she'll say when she finds out I'm in love with Chris. You think she's gonna welcome me with open arms? She's gonna crucify me. And I thought you would stand up for yourself. I'd needed you to stand up for yourself, to give me some clue that it was okay. You didn't. You caved. So I've spent the past four years pretending I'm in love with his sister because I can't stand the thought of my mother saying any of those things about me."

Mack's chest ached at the realization. He had failed Daniel, but not the way he'd thought. Worse. The pain he saw in his son's eyes made his heart hurt.

"And yes," Daniel continued, "I waltzed right in here, tried to upend your life because you seem so amenable. And still, you have no backbone. You don't know how to stand up for yourself. If you did, you wouldn't be agreeing to sell your house, would you?"

Mack nodded. "Actually, I would. Because I'm movin' in with Jeff."

Daniel's eyes went wide as saucers.

For once, the boy was stunned into silence.

IN A WAY, JEFF FELT SORRY FOR Daniel. He'd heard the vicious things people said when they passed judgment, so he understood. Mostly.

"That's the only good thing that's come out of this," Mack continued, his shoulder tense beneath Jeff's hand. "You pushin' me sent me back to where I've belonged all this time. I'm just damn lucky he was still there, that I hadn't lost him forever."

Jeff squeezed Mack's shoulder, then dropped his hand. He honestly hadn't intended to get in the middle of this. He'd stopped by to talk to Mack before he went on duty. It was what he'd done for years when they were together, and he fully intended to add it back into his routine going forward.

"So yes," Mack continued, "I'm sellin' the house, but I'm not sellin' the bar, and I'm damn sure not movin' to Austin. As for what that means for our relationship, I'll leave that up to you. I just want you to know, I would've stood by you, Daniel. I would've backed you no matter what. My love for you has always been unconditional, and I've spent the past four years feeling as though I'd failed you in every way. You didn't need to manipulate me."

At least Daniel looked remorseful, if not a little angry.

When neither of them spoke, Jeff tapped Mack on the shoulder. "I'm goin' in to work. I'll see you at home after?"

Mack slowly turned, his chest rising and falling rapidly. "Yes. I'll be there after I close up."

Before Jeff could turn toward the door, Mack surprised him by grabbing his arm and tugging him forward. Two big hands cupped his face seconds before Mack's lips covered his. It was a brief kiss, but it lingered long enough for Jeff to feel the emotion being delivered in it. He smiled and pressed his forehead to Mack's.

"If you get home before I do, there's meatloaf in the fridge."

Mack chuckled softly. "Okay."

As Jeff walked out of the bar, he was aware of the way Chris and Daniel were staring at him, and while he didn't really care, he couldn't help but wonder what they were thinking.

After a slow Monday night, Jeff was glad to call it a night a little after three in the morning. For the first time in a damn long time, he was excited to go home, knowing Mack would be waiting for him. That was one of the things he'd hated most, coming home to an empty house. Ever since Teddy passed, it had gotten worse. There for a while, he'd considered getting another dog, but he hadn't been able to bring himself to do it. Jeff knew he would never be able to replace those he loved. Not Mack, not Teddy.

He found Mack in the kitchen stirring a pot of noodles on the stove.

"You too good for my meatloaf?" he teased. "What're you makin'?"

Mack smiled over at him. "Wasn't in the mood." He lifted the fork he was using. "I'm makin' spaghetti."

"That explains the garlic stinkin' up the place. Do I have time to change?"

"Change, yes," Mack told him. "Shower, no. We'll do that after."

Smiling to himself, Jeff made his way to their bedroom, and he realized his steps were a little bit lighter because it was theirs once more. No, Mack hadn't technically moved in yet, but he knew it wouldn't be long. Last night, they'd made a list of all of Mack's things—what he wanted to bring, what he wanted to toss—and before he went to the bar last night, Jeff had shifted his clothes around, ensuring Mack had half of the closet and three drawers in the dresser.

After securing his weapon in the gun safe in his nightstand, Jeff changed out of his uniform into a pair of sweatpants and a T-shirt. When he returned to the kitchen, Mack was dishing the spaghetti onto plates, adding chili—Mack was not a fan of sauce—then a slice of garlic bread for each of them. While Jeff grabbed silverware, Mack doused his food with Parmesan and carried the plates to the table.

"So, is it safe to ask how things went after I left?" he asked when they both sat.

"Honestly, I don't know." Mack stared back at him. "I'm not sure Daniel can even rationalize what he did anymore. He kept sayin' he wanted to push me because he didn't believe I loved anything enough to fight for it."

"But he never saw what was right in front of his face? That you loved him more than everything else?"

Mack's face fell and he set his fork down. "I am so goddamn sorry," he rasped. "I never meant—"

Jeff reached out and touched Mack's hand. "I'm not makin' accusations here, Mack. Daniel's your son. You love him. Trust me, I get that. I honestly can't say I would've done anything differently if Kennedy had backed me into that corner."

"She never would have."

"Maybe not, but she's not gay, either. You know as well as I do that it's not easy to live out and proud. There is always gonna be someone who looks down at us, someone who's disgusted. Unfortunately for Daniel, he's feared that person would be his own mother."

"Meredith wouldn't do that," Mack said. "Not to him."

"There's no guarantee, and Daniel couldn't deal with that risk, so he set out on a different path. Probably lost sight of the big picture long ago." Jeff picked up his fork, twirled it into his spaghetti. "Now eat because I could really use that shower."

A smile formed on Mack's face, and some of the tension escaped the air. They ate while Jeff told him about his night, how they'd been called out to Athena Jeffries' house because she was insistent someone had broken in. She'd been right, but the cat burglar had literally been a cat, so all was safe in Coyote Ridge for one more night.

"Are you finished?" Mack asked when Jeff set his fork down.

"I'm done."

"Good." That wicked gleam came into Mack's eyes when he stood and held his hand out. "I say we move this party to the shower."

There was something to be said for making love in a shower. Warm water, soapy hands, and naked bodies tended to function rather well in that environment. The bamboo stool Jeff had acquired a couple of years ago had come in handy, too. Especially when Mack took a seat and proceeded to rock his world with his very skilled mouth. Of course, Jeff had to call a halt to it before he came, because he had something else in mind for the man he loved.

After drying them both, he led Mack into the bedroom, grabbed the lube from the nightstand drawer, and handed it over.

"Me?" Mack asked, eyes wide.

"Oh, did I not make myself clear?" Jeff teased, stepping in close and running his lips over Mack's collarbone. "You're gonna lube me up and ride me. Think you can handle that?"

For the next half hour, Mack proved just how much stamina they both still had.

Chapter Ten

Friday, January 31, 2020

"WHY EXACTLY ARE WE SPENDIN' DATE NIGHT at Moonshiners?" Kylie asked as Travis opened the door to the bar.

"To celebrate," he said simply.

"Celebrate what?"

"Curious tonight, ain't she?" Travis asked Gage.

Kylie stopped, causing Travis to nearly plow over her. She spun around and stared up at him, her finger poking in his chest. "Just so you know, you, Mr. Walker, are using up valuable time. Time we could be using to do other things."

"What sort of other things?" he asked, sliding his hand under her hair and cupping the back of her neck.

"Well, I imagine they would involve me wearing less clothing."

Travis let his gaze rake down her. The short black dress she wore revealed just enough to stimulate the imagination.

"I'm sure I could work around the dress if I need to," he promised.

Kylie laughed, her blue eyes twinkling as she smacked his chest. He caught her hand, kissed her knuckles, then led her to a table near the door.

"So who summoned us tonight?" she asked, clearly not giving up. "Kaleb?"

"Nope."

"Zane?"

"Nope."

"Ethan?"

"Uh-uh."

Kylie's eyebrows lowered, something she did when she was thinking too hard.

"Sawyer?"

Travis shook his head.

"Braydon?"

"Nope."

"Brendon?"

He smiled. "Not any of my brothers, darlin'."

"Kaden and Keegan? Did they finally get up the nerve to ask Bristol out?"

Travis laughed. "If they did, why would they want us to tag along?"

Not to mention, Bristol was with Kaden, Keegan, and Beau's mother, the four of them attempting to corral the kids at Travis's folks' place so Curtis and Lorrie could join the celebration tonight. At least for a little while.

"Is it just me or does there seem to be some tension between them?" Kylie asked. "Something seems off since Christmas."

Truth be told, Travis wasn't paying much attention these days, but now that she'd mentioned it, he was sure he'd find a way to get up in their business sooner or later.

Gage joined them, carrying three beers. He set them down, then eased into a chair beside Kylie.

"He won't tell me," she pouted as she leaned toward him, planting her hand on his chest and giving him those puppy dog eyes. "Do you know?"

"If I did, I promise I'd tell you."

That was clearly not what she'd been hoping to hear, but before she could launch into more questions, the door opened, effectively distracting her.

For the next hour, people began piling in. Kaleb and Zoey, Zane and V, Ethan and Beau, Braydon and Jessie, Sawyer and Kennedy, Brendon and Cheyenne, and Curtis and Lorrie. Chester had come, so had Greyson and Olivia, Jaxson, CJ and the rest of the volunteer fire department. Robert, Mack's brother, had come in and led his young wife right to the bar, evidently wanting a front-row seat. Rex and Jack finally arrived, along with Rafe, who was brooding in the corner, his full attention on Bailey Weber, Mack's trusty waitress. As usual, Mack was behind the bar, only he was smiling for the first time in a long damn time.

Of course, there was one person who was glaringly absent. Travis had honestly hoped that Daniel would show up tonight because Kennedy had personally extended the invitation.

"So what's the big surprise?" Kylie asked, leaning toward him once more.

Travis curled his arm over her shoulder and pulled her close so he could whisper in her ear. "If you ask me that one more time, I'm gonna take you to that little office in the back and give you a distraction."

Kylie laughed, once more smacking his chest. "You wouldn't dare."

He eyed her, ensuring she saw the promise. Before he could go caveman on her and toss her over his shoulder, the door opened and the sheriff stepped inside.

Travis met the man's gaze and nodded. Kennedy had come through for her father, gathering everyone who was important to Mack and getting them there for this very special occasion. Granted, Kennedy hadn't bothered to tell anyone the reason for their coming. Well, anyone except Travis, because he wouldn't commit until she did. Of course, she'd only agreed to tell him if he promised to help. Which he did.

And here they were.

Finally.

———

THE INSTANT TRAVIS WALKER STEPPED INTO THE bar, Mack had suspected something was going on. And with every Walker who filed in behind him, his hackles had risen. Something was definitely going down, though for the life of him, he couldn't figure out what. However, he did seem to be entertaining the masses tonight, all eyes watching his every move.

He hadn't really gotten antsy until Robert had showed up with his wife in tow. He couldn't remember the last time his brother had come to the bar, but he had to admit, he was happy to see him there. But Curtis and Lorrie's arrival had made his Spidey senses tingle, and Mack knew he looked like a man who was waiting for the guillotine to fall.

When the door opened and Jeff walked in, Mack breathed a little easier. The sheriff had promised he would stop by when he got a chance, and just seeing him made Mack relax a little. Since his man was on duty tonight, Mack retrieved a Coke from the fridge and poured it into a glass, earning a thank you and a wink. He went back to work, filling orders, listening to the chatter, and smiling to himself.

Right up until the entire bar went eerily silent.

His eyes shot to the door, but there was no one there, no new arrival who had caught everyone off guard.

Confused, Mack glanced around, realizing all eyes were once again on him.

"What?" he asked, grabbing a dish towel and wiping his hands. "Do I have somethin' on my face?"

That earned him a few chuckles and a bunch of smiles.

Then Jeff disengaged from the conversation he'd been having with Robert and walked over to meet Mack at the side of the bar.

Mack frowned. "Everything all right?"

"Actually, everything's damn near perfect," Jeff said, his voice ringing clearly through the bar. "However, that could take a turn depending on your answer."

"My answer?" Mack motioned for the door to the back room. "Do you want to go back there and talk?"

Jeff shook his head. "Oh, no. What I have to ask, I can do right here."

Completely baffled, Mack stared at Jeff. "What are—"

"Michael Evan Schwartz"—Jeff slowly went down to one knee before him—"will you marry me?"

Mack felt every single eye in the room, could feel the collective breath being held, but the only things he heard were the rapid thump of his own heart, the blood rushing in his ears. He was grateful for his beard because it likely disguised the heat making his cheeks flame. But despite the embarrassment of being in the spotlight, there was only one thing he was focused on. The man kneeling before him, the only man he'd ever loved with all of his heart, the man he wanted to spend the rest of his life with.

"Mack?" Jeff asked, the word wobbling on his tongue. "Please don't leave me hangin'."

Clearly he'd waited a bit too long to answer.

Smiling, Mack held up a finger to signal he needed a minute. He then tucked his other hand in his pocket and dug around to find what he'd been stowing there for the past three days, ever since he'd picked it up at the jeweler.

He noticed a hint of panic on Jeff's face seconds before he said, "Of course I'll marry you. But I think it should go on record that I'd planned to ask that very same question."

The room exploded in laughter when Mack held up the ring, ensured everyone could see it. He took Jeff's hand and pulled him to his feet. Not caring that all eyes were on them, Mack tugged him closer, kissed him square on the lips.

When he finally released him, Jeff leaned in, his mouth next to Mack's ear. "Justice of the peace, Monday afternoon. I'm not waitin' any longer to make you mine, Michael Schwartz."

"I'll be there," he promised.

At two o'clock, when the last customer had left, Mack locked the front doors and shot Jeff a text, asking him to stop by when he could. Since it would take roughly an hour to get through his closing checklist, he figured Jeff would be able to spare him a few minutes before he left. If not, he'd wait for him at home.

God, he loved that. Home. With Jeff.

As he strolled through the space, tossing the hidden bottles into the trash and stowing chairs on the tops of tables, he found himself humming. It was likely the reason he didn't hear the knock on the front doors until it became an insistent banging. He rushed over, shoved in the key.

"I thought you'd come in the back—" Mack's words died when he saw Daniel standing outside in the cold drizzle.

He stepped back, motioned for his son to come inside before locking the doors again.

"Everything okay?" Mack had left Daniel several voicemails and numerous texts since their showdown on Monday, and they'd all gone unanswered.

"No," Daniel said softly. "It's not."

Mack stepped behind the bar, retrieved a Coke, and offered it to Daniel. He got the feeling his son was working up to a conversation, and the last thing he wanted to do was derail it.

Daniel took a seat at the bar, accepted the can, his eyes locking on Mack's left hand. More specifically, the band that now decorated his ring finger.

"I'm sorry I wasn't here tonight. Kennedy asked me to come and … I couldn't."

Mack nodded, though he didn't understand.

"I didn't think I deserved to be here," Daniel continued. "Not after all the shit I've pulled."

Frowning, Mack moved out from behind the bar. "Daniel—"

"No, wait." Daniel stared at his hands clasping the red can. "I owe you an apology and I know that won't be enough. What I've done … it's unforgivable."

"Nothing's unforgivable," Mack told him, putting his hand on his shoulder.

Daniel shook his head. "I fucked up. Royally. And I was so close to ruining your life completely." He sucked in a ragged breath. "Chris left me. On Monday. He had no idea what I was doing, or why. When he found out … I guess I deserve it. After what I did."

Unable to help himself, Mack stepped closer, pulled Daniel in for a hug.

His son's shoulders shook, so Mack held him until he settled. While he didn't condone Daniel's actions, he wouldn't hold them against him.

"I'm sorry, Dad. I don't expect you to forgive me."

"I do," he whispered.

When Daniel pulled back, Mack released him, stepping away and giving him a moment to collect himself. Daniel was like him in that way, rarely showing emotion and not wanting it to become a spectacle.

"I haven't told Mom," he finally said. "Not sure I will."

Mack understood that, too. Even before he'd ended things with Jeff, they hadn't been out of the closet by choice. They'd kept their relationship secret for many reasons, but mostly because they'd been scared.

Now … well, now, Mack wasn't willing to hide from anyone. He wanted to live out the rest of the days with Jeff, and he would proudly stand behind that choice. As far as he was concerned, if people didn't like it, it wasn't their business in the first fucking place.

"When you do decide to tell her, I'll be glad to go with you," Mack offered.

Daniel's eyes slammed into his. "You would do that? After…"

"I told you, boy, I'd walk through fire for you. Will I uproot my life at this point? No. You were right, I should've stood up for what I wanted. In my defense, you've always been my weakness. When you disappeared from my life, I was lost for a long time. I'd looked forward to every weekend I got to spend with you when you were little. I still look forward to those, though they're rare. So, if you want me to stand behind you, to have your back, you can bet your ass I'll be there for you."

There were tears in Daniel's eyes. "Not sure it's even necessary now. Chris's gone."

"If your love's real, he won't be gone completely. Perhaps you'll have to do some groveling, but that's part of it." Mack held Daniel's stare. "But take my advice. Don't wait too long. Not everyone finds the love that can stand the test of time. If you have, you better grab on and never let go."

Epilogue

Monday, February 3, 2020

THEY'D DONE IT.

Jeff stood in the kitchen, staring down at his left hand and the band circling his finger. He couldn't stop smiling, remembering how he and Mack had stood before the justice of the peace, Kennedy at his side, Daniel at Mack's, their kids there to bear witness to the nuptials.

The ceremony had taken only a few minutes, but they were the minutes Jeff would remember for the rest of his days.

"So, Sheriff, I was wonderin' somethin'."

Jeff turned as Mack's voice drew closer. "What's that?"

"We never talked about who'd take whose name."

"No, we didn't," Jeff admitted. "I didn't think you'd want to change your name."

Mack grinned. "So you assumed you'd be the one to change yours, huh? I think Mack Endsley sounds pretty damn good. Then again, Jeff Schwartz has a nice ring to it."

Jeff smiled. "It does, sure. We could always hyphenate."

Mack suddenly shook his head, stepping in close and taking Jeff's hand. As he'd done on their way out of the courthouse, Mack's thumb brushed over the wedding band on Jeff's finger.

"No hyphenating," he whispered. "I'd be honored to take your name if you'll let me."

His chest filled with love, so much he wondered how he could even contain it all.

"Hopefully you will let me," Mack continued, his eyes glittering with mischief. "Since I've already made it official."

"You did?"

Mack's big hand curled around the back of his head, fingers twining in his hair. "It seemed the right thing to do."

Jeff swallowed as he leaned in, pressed his lips to Mack's. The hand at the back of his head held him firmly in place.

"Somethin' else seems like the right thing to do, too," Mack said, his lips shifting to Jeff's neck.

"And what would that be?" Jeff inhaled sharply when Mack's other hand dipped into the waistband of his jeans.

"Consummate, of course."

Of course.

So they did.

And for the next few days, they also christened every single room in their house.

If you're interested in knowing more about Kaden, Keegan and Bristol, keep reading.

Kaden & Keegan
(The Walkers of Coyote Ridge, 9)

Available now.

Chapter One

KEEGAN WALKER STARED AT HIS TWIN, DOING his damnedest to get the man to come over to his way of thinking. Being as he'd been working on Kaden for the better part of ten minutes, it wasn't looking good for him.

"All right. What about a bakery?"

"Coyote Ridge already has a bakery," Kaden countered.

"Pet store?"

"No."

"Gym?"

"No."

"Vape shop?"

Kaden shot him a *get real* look. "No."

"Thrift shop?" Of course, that had Keegan doing his rendition of Macklemore's "Thrift Shop." "I'm gonna *pop* some *tags* … only got twenty *dollas* in my pocket."

A little too much twang, he thought, but not terrible.

"Stick to your day job, Keeg."

Yeah, yeah, yeah. Whatever. "Fine. No thrift shop. What about an arcade?"

Kaden narrowed his eyes in that manner that spoke of disbelief combined with a modicum of concern. "Seriously?"

"Yeah. Seriously." Keegan *was* serious, and he wasn't sure how much clearer he could be. Yet Kaden didn't seem to be on board, hence the reason he was feigning ignorance.

"Is this some sorta midlife crisis?" Kaden questioned, his dark eyebrow lowered at a sharp slant, his incredulity evident.

"First off, we're a long damn way from *midlife*. And two, it's a damn fine idea and you know it."

"Oh, yeah? And who in their right mind is gonna hang out in an arcade? In Coyote Ridge?"

"Just because *you're* old doesn't mean we all are," Keegan argued, staring at the man who was more or less his mirror image. "Have you seen the town lately? They're finally gettin' with the program."

"Yada, yada, I got it," Kaden sniped. "Ever since Rex opened the B and B, blah, blah. I know the spiel, Keeg."

But what a spiel it was. The Double R Bed and Breakfast had been open for a year, and it had proven to be a fruitful venture in just a short time. The big, renovated farmhouse right in the heart of town had been at capacity every weekend since the opening, and it didn't appear they'd be letting up anytime soon. What more could a small-town hotel ask for? Or those who had invested in the project from the jump?

Keegan grinned wide. "Damn good idea, wasn't it? I knew that place would be a helluva investment."

"Frog giggin', cow tippin', and a B and B. What more could Coyote Ridge *possibly* offer?" Kaden grumbled.

"An arcade," Keegan answered, deadpan.

Kaden rolled his eyes again.

Keegan had known his brother would react this way. They might share the same DNA code, but there was no denying their personalities were polar opposite. Kaden had always been the level-headed one, the one who came up with a plan even when a plan wasn't necessary. Keegan was more of the fly-by-the-seat-of-your-pants kinda guy. He tried not to take things too seriously, while Kaden spent more time thinking than actually doing. And sure, Keegan could admit his brother was usually right when it came down to their arguments.

Didn't mean Keegan agreed with his twin. In fact, most of the time they didn't see eye to eye at all.

But...

Yes, but. Backing Rex Sharpe in the bed-and-breakfast had been a stellar idea if he did say so himself. And now, who was to say an arcade couldn't bring some life to this sleepy little town? Of course, Keegan was only considering it because his true dream couldn't be realized yet. It had always been his goal to own a ranch, but without one available to acquire, that was unfortunately on the back burner.

"Well"—Keegan lifted his coffee mug, offered his brother a casual one-shoulder shrug—"I think it's a smart idea. Think about all the things Coyote Ridge has goin' for it. Just in the time we've been here, they've opened a toy store and a bookstore, right on Main Street. I heard they're plannin' to expand the bookstore to include a coffee shop. An arcade might kick it up a notch."

"I get my coffee at the bakery," Kaden retorted.

"*Options*, Kaden. We're always open for *options*."

"No. No way," Kaden retorted. "I'll admit, I doubted the B and B in the beginning, and it turned out all right, but I'm not at all on board with an arcade."

"Okay, fine," Keegan conceded. "What then? It's not set in stone and the place is still for sale. We can snatch it up, put in somethin' of our own." He leaned in, lowered his voice. "For fuck's sake, everyone else is doin' it. Why can't we?"

"If everyone else was jumpin' off a cliff, would you wanna do that, too, Keeg?"

He grinned. "Damn straight I would."

Those familiar steel-blue eyes glinted with incredulity. "You're serious? You want... *Us*? You and me...?" Kaden exhaled with a sigh and shook his head. "Ain't gonna happen, Keeg."

Keegan chuckled. He happened to enjoy getting his brother riled. Especially first thing in the morning.

"I'll come up with somethin'," he told his twin. "You just wait." Although he certainly wasn't giving up on the arcade.

Kaden challenged him back with a simple tilt of his eyebrows upward.

Keegan knew that look. Kaden thought he was off his rocker. And perhaps he was, but hey, everyone else seemed to be making their mark on this town. Why couldn't they?

Kaden leaned back, allowed the waitress to set his plate down in front of him. "Thanks." He turned his full attention to Keegan. "Might I remind you, we've got enough on our plates."

Keegan smiled at the waitress. "Thanks, doll." He peered over at his brother. "What? With Walker Demo? That's gonna be our claim to fame?" It was his turn to shake his head. "In case you didn't notice, it just kicked over leadership again."

Granted, that was because Reese Tavoularis had moved on to the governor's task force, another brainchild of their cousin Travis Walker. In Reese's place, Autumn Jameson—one of Travis's many cousins on his mother's side—had come on board to run things. She'd been in her new role for nearly a month, and to his surprise, she was doing pretty darn well. He was tempted to say she could pinpoint an issue with an engine faster than he could. But that didn't change the fact that even the family business didn't seem all that stable.

"What about the time we're puttin' in on the ranch?" Kaden asked.

"Key word there bein' *the*. *The* ranch infers that it doesn't belong to us."

As much as he enjoyed working on the Walker ranch, which belonged to Uncle Curtis and Aunt Lorrie, it had always been a dream of his to have one of his own. And yes, Keegan was keeping his eyes open for that opportunity. If it were to arise tomorrow, he'd drop every damn thing else and follow his dream. Until then…

Silence settled between them as Kaden covered his scrambled eggs in tabasco sauce. Rather than stir him up more, Keegan took a sip of his orange juice, stared at his pancakes. He always had pancakes. Every damn day. Why? At what point in his thirty-seven years had he gotten so damn … boring?

"Are you really serious about this? Openin' a place of our own?" Kaden finally asked, his voice lowered.

"Hell, I don't know. I'm just…" He met his twin's eyes. "I'm tired of watchin' everyone else doin' their thing while we settle for bein' along for the ride."

Kaden sighed.

Keegan sat up straight, picked up his fork. "Tell you what. I'm gonna stuff my face with these pancakes and we can pretend this conversation never happened. Deal?"

Kaden's blue-gray eyes locked on his face, but Keegan didn't flinch. He knew how he sounded. Petulant, whiny, sullen. Take your pick.

In his defense, Keegan had always allowed Kaden to make the final decisions. Sure, he threw in his two cents, like where they were gonna put down roots. His choice had always been Coyote Ridge, and since they were metaphorically attached at the hip, where one of them went, the other followed. When they arrived here, they'd thought it would be a fruitful venture. Years later, although they'd technically settled in, they weren't completely settled.

"Fine," Kaden huffed, grabbing his coffee mug. "Let's talk to Travis. Get his thoughts."

Great. Go to the man with the plan and tell him what? That they didn't have a plan? Yeah, no thank you. Their cousin Travis was not just *paving* the way here in Coyote Ridge, he *was* the way. Hell, after Travis's daughter was kidnapped a few weeks back, a task force governing the state of Texas had been formed to search for other missing people. Thank the good Lord, Kate had been located and returned seemingly unharmed two painfully long days after she went missing, but still. Guy had some serious pull. Not to mention, half the town went to Travis for advice. Keegan didn't want to be another in that long line.

Keegan sipped his juice, glared at his pancakes.

They finished their breakfast in silence, although it was obvious Kaden's mind was running a million miles a minute. That was the way his twin's brain worked. Whenever Keegan planted an idea, his brother would veto it immediately, then spend considerable time mulling it over until he came to a final decision. Generally, Keegan would go along with whatever his brother wanted, because truth was, Keegan was the laid-back one. Most things he could simply take or leave. Didn't matter. But something hadn't been sitting well with him lately.

While living and working in this small town had always been a dream of his, there was only one teeny tiny problem... They hadn't really put down roots. When Keegan took stock of what they had to call their own ... besides their trucks, there wasn't much of anything.

Take the house they occupied, for instance. Someone else's. Technically, it was now just one of seven separate structures Curtis had built for his boys when they were old enough to venture out on their own. Originally, it had been Kaleb's place. Then it was Jared's for a bit. Now it was theirs until they figured out what they wanted to do.

To buy or not to buy? Coyote Ridge or bust? For the moment, their options were open although real estate in Coyote Ridge was scarce and what did come available was usually snatched up within hours of being listed. If it ever made it to listing at all. Just like the building on Main Street. If they didn't make their play, it would be gone before they knew it. There wasn't even an apartment to be had. Not that Keegan had any desire to live in an apartment. He preferred wide-open spaces.

Sure, he loved Coyote Ridge. Had since he was a kid, when their parents would bring them and their brothers and sister down to visit their aunts and uncles. He remembered one summer—they were probably twelve, maybe thirteen—his brothers and sister all ganged up on their parents, tried to convince them to move to the small town their father had grown up in. Their parents won in the end, determined to hold down the fort in El Paso, but they'd all talked about moving here eventually.

Their oldest brother was the first to take the leap, relocating to Coyote Ridge permanently. Jared had fled a bad situation only to have it all turn around for the best once he settled down here. Of course, Quinn and Eve had rolled in only a month ago, with Wesley promising to pull up the rear sometime in the next year. At the very least, Wesley had promised to make it down here at some point during the holidays. Keegan was looking forward to seeing their overachieving doctor brother as well as their parents.

Even having his family close wasn't doing what it used to though. Keegan wanted something more.

Then again, perhaps that didn't have anything to do with the house they lived in or the jobs they held or the hobbies they'd picked up along the way. In most ways, they had the life they'd hoped for. Perhaps his settling-down issue had more to do with a some*one*, not necessarily a some*thing*.

That, of course, was Kaden's fault. His twin was still adamant they would eventually have the big wedding and greet some sweet young thing at the end of the aisle where they would vow to love endlessly, blah, blah, fucking blah. Keegan was no longer disillusioned in that area. Been there, done that. Twice. Another ride on the merry-go-round that was shitty relationships? No fucking thank you.

Unfortunately, he was starting to suspect Kaden had a specific woman in mind.

Did he still want to share women with his twin? Damn straight. He didn't know any other way. Their desire to share women between them was something that had come naturally since they were old enough to don a condom. Then it had been sealed thanks to Mrs. Whitley, the sexy housewife who'd turned two horny teenagers into men. Some found their untraditional need an abomination, but that had always been the way it was for them, and Keegan wasn't the sort to make excuses for it.

It was the marriage part he wasn't on board with. Nothing permanent, either. Fucking for the sake of fucking, that was his motto. Why, you ask? Well, that was because their attempts at happily ever after had blown up in their faces not once but twice in their history. Thank the good Lord, they'd never made it to the altar either time, but that had been the plan.

He was still on board with shagging the same chick, but he was no longer interested in seeing if it would lead to something more. It wouldn't. Might as well steer clear of the heartache.

Which was another reason Keegan was content to live in Coyote Ridge. He saw the way people treated Travis, Kylie, and Gage. They certainly weren't abominations and they were making the ménage à trois work. Of course, that was a different version of what Keegan and Kaden engaged in. Travis was in love with both Kylie and Gage, he was intimate with both of them, while Keegan and Kaden merely wanted to bang a willing, sexy woman from both ends. At the same time.

Crude, yeah, he could see that.

And yes, he was jaded.

So fucking what.

Kaden's cell phone rang, drawing Keegan from his rambling thoughts.

His brother snatched the phone off the table. "What's up, Trav?"

Keegan watched Kaden's face, waited to see what emergency they were being dragged into now. For whatever reason, they were the go-tos when it came to helping out Curtis's branch of the Walker family tree.

"Absolutely. We can run by there now, take them to the daycare. No problem."

Keegan grinned. Looked as though they were on chauffeur duty again.

When Kaden hung up, he grabbed his napkin, wiped his mouth, and signaled the waitress over.

"What was that about?"

Kaden reviewed the check, pulled out some cash. "Travis needs us to run by his house and pick up Kade, Avery, and Maddox. Asked us to drop them off at the daycare."

"Somethin' wrong?"

Kaden got to his feet. "Said Haden isn't feelin' well. Runnin' a fever. Kylie's hesitant to get him outta the house."

"Can't blame her there. What about Kate? She back at school yet?" Keegan asked, hopeful the little darling was finding some normalcy again after her horrific ordeal with the crazy psycho bitch who'd snatched her.

"Not yet. Travis said she's with him at the resort. Gonna take her to Lorrie this afternoon."

Keegan got to his feet, grabbed a five out of his wallet, and tossed it onto the table along with the money his brother left.

"I covered the tip already," Kaden mumbled as they were walking toward the door.

"And I bumped it a little. Now she'll be happy to see us next time we come in."

Kaden smirked. "She's happy to see us already."

Yeah, but Keegan was still on the fence as to whether he was going to attempt to get her phone number or not. Never hurt to be extra nice.

You know, just in case.

HALF AN HOUR LATER, KADEN WAS HOPPING out of the truck while his brother carried on a conversation with the three kids strapped into their car seats in the back seat. Kaden couldn't help it, he was laughing at some ridiculous joke Keegan told. Didn't matter that it was juvenile and rather simple, he still laughed.

Kaden had to admit, he was a tad jealous of how easily Keegan got along with the little ones. His twin was the guy all the kids wanted to be around, the one they chased over and under the jungle gym, shot with water guns on Sunday afternoons, hunted Easter eggs with, opened presents with. In recent months, Keegan had even claimed Beau's title belt as the favorite uncle, although technically they were cousins, not uncles.

Granted, that transition only happened because Beau was ear-deep in dirty diapers of his own with the rowdy triplets. Beau had promised Keegan he would be back to challenge him for the title, but he needed some time to settle in. Kaden had to wonder how true that was because the triple terrors were now one, and Beau was still on hiatus, his return to glory still iffy.

Didn't seem to bother Keegan in the least. In fact, Kaden was pretty sure Keegan was mighty proud of the title.

Funny thing was, Keegan didn't have to try too hard to be the favorite. He was merely good with kids. Kaden, on the other hand, loved the little munchkins, but he didn't have the smooth way that Keegan did. His brother would talk them into damn near anything, including brushing their teeth and eating their vegetables. The guy was a miracle worker.

At one point, Kaden had figured they'd have a houseful of their own rugrats by now, a ranch to raise them on. Some sweet woman sleeping between them, waking them up with a smile, a woman they could love beyond reason, spoil because she deserved it. So far, it hadn't happened, but he hadn't lost faith.

Kaden even had one particular woman in mind, but he found himself trying to navigate a couple of obstacles.

One: Bristol Newton, the sassy daycare owner he'd set his eye on, was proving to be resistant to their charms. A problem Kaden figured could be remedied if he just put his heart into it.

Two: Keegan. His twin was adamantly opposed to happily ever after. According to him, it wasn't possible, so why bother. He did, however, say *just sex* was always on the table.

Kaden didn't really see Bristol as the *just-sex* kinda girl, which brought him around to those obstacles he was still attempting to hurdle.

"Man, y'all are lucky," Keegan was saying when Kaden opened the truck door to help Avery out of her car seat.

"Why? Why are we lucky, Uncle Keeg?" four-year-old Kade asked, smiling widely as Keegan leaned in on the other side of the truck to assist him out.

"Because y'all get to come here," Keegan explained, motioning toward the daycare.

And see Bristol. Kaden kept that thought to himself as he set Avery on her feet because, at three, the little girl was already too independent to be carried.

Kaden took her hand before shutting the rear door. When he reached the front of the truck, Keegan was joining him, one hand firmly held in Kade's, the other arm filled with eighteen-month-old Maddox.

"There's all kinds of cool stuff to play with here," Keegan continued.

Kaden grinned. It was pretty much the same conversation they had anytime they brought one of the kids here. There were currently twenty-three little ones between Curtis and Lorrie's seven sons, the last of the herd—Zane and V's Dustin—born last December. For the first time in years, none of the women were pregnant. And due to being far outnumbered by the short-legged Walkers, Kaden and Keegan were often called in to help out in one capacity or another.

As for the daycare, they'd brought almost all of them here at some point. Keegan had mastered the art of hyping them up to want to go in. On occasion, one would make a mad dash for the door in an attempt to escape, but by the time Kaden was leaving, the kids were always excited. That was Keegan for you.

"There is," Kade assured Keegan with a huge grin. "All *kinds* of stuff."

"That's just not fair," Keegan said as he opened the outer door, allowing Kade and Avery to step in before him, then Kaden. "I wanna play with the cool stuff."

Once inside, they remained in the small vestibule, waiting for the interior doors to be unlocked. No one was allowed in who wasn't on the approved list of visitors, had their fingerprints on file, and knew their specialized code. No exceptions.

Kaden stepped up to the keypad, typed in the six-digit code, pressed his finger to the scanner, and waited.

"Maybe Miss Bristol'll let you play, too," Kade told Keegan, his brow furrowed as he peered up, the spitting image of Travis only in miniature form. "I can ask her."

Keegan's response was a conspiratorial grin and a quick nod.

Kaden chuckled. God, he loved these kids. They were so damn innocent, reminding him of a simpler time. And he felt blessed to have a chance to hang out with his cousins and their little ones on a daily basis. Plus, from time to time, he got to hang with his brother Jared, spend some quality time with his own nephew and niece.

"You do that," Keegan told Kade. "If Miss Bristol says it's cool, maybe we can play for a few minutes."

On more than one occasion, Kaden had had to sit back and watch Keegan build block castles with the little kids. Sometimes he wondered if his twin wouldn't mind spending his day here just so he could do that.

The lock disengaged, allowing them to open the interior door. The instant Kade stepped inside, he released Keegan's hand and began jumping up and down. "Miss Bristol! Miss Bristol!" he squealed.

Bristol Newton peered up from her spot at the desk, her light blue eyes glittering, a smile tilting the corners of her full lips. Clearly Kade knew to wait until he was acknowledged.

She turned in her chair, giving Kade her full attention as she rested her elbows on her knees, leaning toward him. "Good mornin', Kade."

God, he loved that soft twang, the raspy sound of her voice.

Hi, Miss Bristol." Based on the puff of his cheeks, Kade was trying to stifle his energy, but his hands couldn't seem to remain still.

Bristol peered up at them, then back to Kade. She stood and stepped around the desk. "What has you so excited this mornin'?"

"Uncle Keegan wants to play with the cool stuff. Can he? Just for a little while? Purty please?"

While Bristol chatted it up with the kids, Kaden took a minute to admire her. From her shoulder-length brown hair pulled back in a sleek ponytail, to the pink Converse on her feet. She looked all of sixteen, although Kaden knew she'd hit the big three-one earlier in the year. He'd even been invited to the shindig. Of course, he'd come up with an excuse as to why he couldn't go. In his defense, Bristol had been dating some jackass at the time—a temporary thing that had lasted all of two weeks—and he hadn't been keen on subjecting himself to seeing her with another man.

In fact, ever since their incident at Alluring Indulgence last December, it seemed Bristol was attempting to keep them at a distance by flaunting other men. Didn't matter that they never lasted much past a first date and she never shared any stories of hope for something more with the many women in her orbit. If she had, perhaps he would've had to intervene. Since she seemed to be doing what she could to push him and his brother away, he'd been biding his time.

But she was single now.

Very single.

When those glittering eyes lifted to meet his, a wide grin on her face, he was hard-pressed to keep from winking at her, a bad habit he'd acquired when picking up women. Fortunately, he knew better. Bristol was not the sort of woman who would be impressed by a wink and a smile. She was far too smart for that. In fact, she'd rebuked every attempt he'd made to flirt with her in the past. Except for that one alcohol-fueled night. Still, that hadn't deterred him in the least. Of course, he'd thought for sure they'd made inroads with her last Christmas, but he should've known better.

"Well, all right," she told Kade with a chuckle before peering up at Keegan. "I think it'll be fine if Uncle Keegan hangs out for a bit."

"Yay!" Kade squealed, jumping up and down as he grabbed Keegan's hand and jerked him toward the door leading to the inner sanctum.

"Hold up, speedy. Your sister's gonna wanna join us."

Kaden remained in the front office as Keegan keyed his passcode in a secondary keypad and then motioned Avery in front of him, making the little girl giggle as Kade grabbed Avery's hand and took off at a trot toward the back the instant the door opened.

"Sometimes I think you should charge him for bein' here," Kaden told Bristol as he stepped over to the wide window that overlooked the room where the kids congregated, watching his brother pass Maddox off to a waiting teacher.

"I think it's sweet," she said, bending over to jot something down in her notebook before standing tall once more.

The outfit she wore was more for comfort than fashion, he figured, but the woman would've looked damn fine wearing a potato sack. The light blue skinny jeans couldn't have been more formfitting if they'd been painted on. The plus was how they showcased toned legs and a sinful ass while the oversized cream-colored sweatshirt hid the nice curves he knew she rocked on that petite frame.

Truth was, Kaden was usually drawn to leggy women, the ones who were closer to his six foot two inches. Bristol couldn't have been but a few inches over five feet. Still there was something about her that did it for him.

"I'll be sure to tell him you said that." Kaden grinned. "He likes when women call him sweet."

Speaking of sweet, Bristol was sweet enough to cause a toothache and sassy enough to square a man's shoulders. Not to mention, she was as stubborn as she was beautiful. Oddly enough, he didn't even have to wink to make Bristol blush. Despite the fact they'd spent countless hours in her presence, usually at one Walker function or another, he always detected a hint of nerves when she was around them.

"So, will you be attendin' the fall festival?" she asked while they stood watching as a group of kids built a block fort around Keegan.

Fall festival? They'd just had the back to school festival, hadn't they? He did a mental calculation, realized the fall festival was only a few days away. Next weekend, in fact.

"Is it just me or does Coyote Ridge have a festival for everything?"

Bristol smiled up at him, a flash of those pretty white teeth. "I think the mayor's responsible for that."

"It hasn't always been that way?"

"Oh, no." She shook her head. "Not like this, anyway. We've had one or two a year, but only for the past couple of years has it ramped up. It's kinda nice."

Nice wasn't the word he would've used. Saying there was a festival for everything wasn't an exaggeration. Just in the past year, he'd been suckered into attending a Valentine's festival, Founder's Day festival, Easter, Memorial Day, the Kick Off to Summer festival, July Fourth, Back to School, some kind of Ode to Pets festival, and now the town's long-running annual fall festival.

How exactly did anyone get anything done around this place when they spent so much damn time decorating and organizing events?

"I think it's her way of revitalizin' the town," Bristol continued. "Mayor Stewart is all about bringin' the residents together."

Kaden found himself mesmerized by Bristol's glossy pink lips and the twinkle in her eyes. He wanted to kiss those lips again, to slide his tongue along the seam and dip inside, hear her reaction. It had been too damn long since he'd gotten a taste of her.

"Does that mean you'll be attendin'?" he asked, breaking the hold she had over him and forcing his eyes to meet hers.

Bristol grinned. "Of course. Mayor Stewart roped me into it."

"I find it amusin' you refer to her as Mayor Stewart considerin' Bianca's your best friend."

Bristol laughed. "One of them, yes. But I do it because it irritates her."

That made him smile. He liked her sassiness. Kaden only wished she'd turn all that attitude on him sometime.

"Well?" she asked, still staring at him.

Kaden frowned. "Well, what?"

"Can I add you to the list of people attendin'?"

"Depends."

"On?"

Kaden held her stare and offered his best smile. "What's in it for me?"

ACKNOWLEDGMENTS

Of course, I have to thank my wonderfully patient husband who puts up with me every single day. If it wasn't for him and his belief that I could (and can) do this, I wouldn't be writing this today. He has been my backbone, my rock, the very reason I continue to believe in myself. I love you for that, babe.

I also have to thank my street team – Naughty (and nice) Girls – Your unwavering support is something I will never take for granted.

I can't forget my copyeditor, Amy at Blue Otter Editing. Thank goodness I've got you to catch all my punctuation, grammar, and tense errors.

Nicole Nation 2.0 for the constant support and love. You've been there for me from almost the beginning. This group of ladies has kept me going for so long, I'm not sure I'd know what to do without them.

And, of course, YOU, the reader. Your emails, messages, posts, comments, tweets… they mean more to me than you can imagine. I thrive on hearing from you, knowing that my characters and my stories have touched you in some way keeps me going. I've been known to shed a tear or two when reading an email because you simply bring so much joy to my life with your support. I thank you for that.

ABOUT NICOLE EDWARDS

New York Times and *USA Today* bestselling author Nicole Edwards lives in the suburbs of Austin, Texas with her husband and their youngest of three children. The two older ones have flown the coup, while the youngest is in high school. When Nicole is not writing about sexy alpha males and sassy, independent women, she can often be found with a book in hand or attempting to keep the dogs happy. You can find her hanging out on social media and interacting with her readers - even when she's supposed to be writing.

Want to know what's coming next? Or how about see some fun stuff related to Nicole's books? You can find these, as well as tons of other stuff on Nicole's website. You can also find A Day in the Life blog posts, which are short stories about your favorite characters, as well as exclusive contests by joining Nicole Nation on Nicole's website. To join, simply click **Log In | Register** in the menu.

If you're interested in keeping up to date on any new releases and preorders, you can sign up for Nicole's notification newsletter. This only goes out when she's got important information to share.

Want a simple, fast way to get updates on new releases? Sign up for text messaging. If you are in the U.S. simply text NICOLE to 64600 or sign up on her website. She promises not to spam your phone. This is just her way of letting you know what's happening because Nicole knows you're busy, but if you're anything like her, you always have your phone on you.

CONNECT WITH NICOLE

Website: NicoleEdwardsAuthor.com

Facebook: /Author.Nicole.Edwards

Instagram: NicoleEdwardsAuthor

Twitter: @NicoleEAuthor

Want to see where it all started?

Keep reading for an excerpt from

Curtis

Prologue

"POP!"

Curtis Walker glanced around, looking for the face of the person calling him. He recognized the voice, but for the life of him, he couldn't place it. The last few hours had left him jittery and frustrated, making it damn near impossible to think about anything except his wife.

Lorrie.

God, baby, please be okay.

His chest hurt so much that it was difficult to breathe. His lungs felt ten times too small. As though a band was cinched tightly around his ribs, squeezing, suffocating.

Damn it.

He needed air. Needed … something.

A firm hand touched his shoulder, and he focused long enough to realize his oldest son was standing at his side.

Shit. Where am I?

"Dad? You okay?"

No. No, he wasn't. Not even a little bit.

Then it all came back to him in a rush of noise and light mingling with the stench of disinfectant and disease. He was in the emergency room waiting area because they had taken Lorrie back for some tests. He remembered the nurse had kindly asked him to wait out here because he was a nervous wreck and he was making the doctor uneasy. At first, he'd considered arguing—for a brief moment, even throwing a punch at the surly doctor—but when he'd looked down at his wife, so pale, so weak, lying in that bed, her lips thin, eyes dim from the pain she was enduring, he had relented.

And yeah, damn it, he was a fucking nervous wreck. How could he not be? His wife was sick. Sicker than he'd ever seen her in her life, and he'd been by her side through plenty of illnesses over the past fifty plus years they'd been together.

"Where's Mom?" Travis asked, his tone gruff, his face a stony mask of concern.

Curtis met his oldest son's gaze, those hard, blue-gray eyes identical to his own. "Tests," he forced out, noticing that Travis's wife, Kylie, his husband, Gage, and their daughter, Kate, were with him.

"Dad, you need to sit down," Curtis's daughter-in-law stated firmly, her hand curling around his arm as she led him toward one of the empty chairs.

He hadn't even realized he was standing. *Shit.*

He needed to pull himself together.

Although he towered over Kylie by a solid foot, outweighed her by God only knew how much, it seemed she had more strength in her hand than he had in his entire body.

Lorrie.

"Breathe," Kylie stated delicately. "Just breathe."

Not so easy when there were ten tons of emotions sitting on his chest. Not knowing what was going on with Lorrie made it damn near impossible to function, but he forced himself to draw air into his lungs, exhaling slowly.

"Where're your brothers?" Curtis asked Travis, doing his best to clear the fog from his head.

"They're on the way. I called them as soon as I hung up with you. Did the doctor say anything before they sent you out here?"

Curtis shook his head. Hell, he couldn't remember half of what the doctor had said. "Something about infection…"

Travis's hand was once again on Curtis's shoulder, giving him comfort. "From the kidney stone?"

"They said that shouldn't have caused it." In layman's terms, the stone was gone, so technically it was no longer an issue.

Oh, God. Curtis put his hands on his face, tried to gather his composure, but it was futile. The riot of emotion was tearing him apart. He just needed to be by Lorrie's side. It was the one place on earth that he belonged, and they had sent him away. Banished him to the godforsaken waiting room.

He knew Lorrie would be fine on her own, but he wasn't so sure he'd be fine without her.

"Hey, Trav. Pop."

Curtis looked up to see more of his boys coming toward him. Ethan and his husband, Beau, along with Kaleb and his wife, Zoey. Not far behind were Sawyer and his wife, Kennedy. He knew the rest would be along shortly, especially if Travis had told them that their mother was sick.

"What sort of tests are they doing?" Kylie asked, her hand gently resting on his forearm.

"Blood tests and a CT scan." At least that was what he thought they'd said. He really wasn't sure.

"What happened?" Kennedy questioned.

Curtis sat up straight, gripped the arms of the chair, and took another deep breath. He tried to ignore the incessant pounding of his heart as he looked at his daughter-in-law, then around at the others. "She woke up this mornin', said she felt horrible. She couldn't eat, and if she tried, she couldn't hold anything down. Her temperature was one-oh-three..." God, she'd looked so pitiful. It had broken his heart to realize he couldn't do a damn thing to help her, either.

Ethan squatted down in front of Curtis, placing his hand on Curtis's knee. "When did this start?"

"When she went to bed last night, she said she didn't feel well. Thought maybe she was coming down with the flu."

"The flu?" Ethan frowned. "But she's been better since Friday?"

Curtis nodded. "For a bit, yes. Then this morning, her skin was kinda ashy. Finally, she told me to get her to the hospital." That was when he'd known it was bad. Lorrie hated hospitals, so for her to suggest it meant there was a serious problem.

"Be right back." Travis patted Curtis's shoulder, then headed over to the nurse's desk as more people moved toward him.

Braydon and Jessie, Brendon and Cheyenne, Zane and Vanessa. Now all his boys and their significant others were there, along with his nephew, Jared, and Jared's son, Derrick. Not far behind them, Curtis saw his sister, Maryanne, and her husband, Thomas.

Looked as though word had gotten out.

"I need to see her," Curtis mumbled to himself, not thinking about all the people who where there watching him lose his shit.

"You will," Kylie assured him. "Travis'll make sure of it."

"She'll be okay, Pop," Ethan said, his voice low. Curtis heard the concern in his boy's tone, though. He knew everyone was as worried as he was. Lorrie was the backbone of their family. Without her...

No, he wasn't going to think about that. She was going to be fine.

She *had* to be.

LORRIE WALKER FELT LIKE CRAP WARMED OVER. Her entire body hurt and she had no idea why. It was as though every fiber of her being was being pricked with tiny needles, then squeezed with pliers. She couldn't stop vomiting, either, but they'd given her something to help with that, or so they'd said. The only thing she wanted to do was sleep until she could wake up and be well again.

They'd been poking and prodding her for the past couple of hours in an attempt to figure out what was going on with her body, but no one seemed to know. And the worst of it was, they had sent Curtis out into the waiting room because he'd been looming over them, making the medical staff nervous. She hadn't wanted him to leave, but she knew it would be best for the doctors and for Curtis if he didn't have to sit and watch.

Now that the CT scan had been done and she'd given more blood than she'd thought she had in her veins, Lorrie was settled into the bed, and they had promised they would go get him, but twenty minutes had passed, and she could hardly keep her eyes open. Still no Curtis.

When the bubbly blond nurse walked in, Lorrie shifted her legs, trying to get comfortable. "Is my husband coming?"

"Oh, right. I'm so sorry, Mrs. Walker. I'll go get him in just a minute. You should probably get some rest in the meantime."

For most of her sixty-seven years, Lorrie had been described as kindhearted. Non-confrontational. Loving even. And yes, she was usually all of those things, including the easygoing woman everyone suspected her to be, but there were a few things in the world guaranteed to set her off. One surefire way was if someone messed with her boys. Another was when it was clear they were trying to keep her away from Curtis—or vice versa. At that point, the gloves came off and a different side of her came out. A side most people didn't want to see.

This nice young woman should've been warned. Too late now.

"You need to go get him," Lorrie said, keeping her tone as polite as she could while she breathed through the pain that was currently tearing apart her insides.

"We will, Mrs. Walker. Just close your eyes and rest."

Lorrie smiled, and based on the way the nurse was looking at her, she knew it wasn't a pleasant one. "I'm only gonna say this one time. And it's more of a warning for you than anything else. If my husband finds out that you're purposely keeping him away from me, the outcome is going to be unlike anything you've *ever* seen before."

And heaven help them all if her boys were out there, too.

The men in her life did not take kindly to someone attempting to keep her away from them. Especially Curtis.

The woman's smile faltered, her forehead creasing. "We understand, but—"

"No, I really don't think that you do." If she did, she wouldn't be standing there gawking at her.

"We thought it might be best if you got a little rest without him here."

Lorrie plastered a fake smile on her face. "I highly suggest you don't tell *him* that."

Lord have mercy. Was it that difficult to understand?

Thankfully, the nurse nodded and rushed out of the room. Within a couple of minutes, Curtis was walking in, his face hard, his beautiful blue-gray eyes reflecting the fear she'd expected to see in them. She hated that he worried so much, but the truth was, she was worried, too. Never had she felt like this before, and she couldn't even pinpoint exactly what the problem was. She hurt *everywhere*.

"What did they say?" Curtis asked, his voice deep but soft as he leaned over and kissed her forehead.

"Something about high white blood cell counts from the preliminary tests," she told him, trying to remember exactly what they'd said. She was having a hard time focusing as it was. Nodding toward the IV in her arm, she continued, "They've put me on antibiotics while they wait for more tests to come back."

Curtis eased into the chair beside her bed and rested his hand over hers.

"I'm so tired," she told him.

"I know, darlin'. Close your eyes and rest. I'm right here."

"You won't leave me?"

"Not in this lifetime."

Knowing he meant every word, Lorrie succumbed to sleep, instantly drifting off, knowing Curtis would keep her safe. Just as he always had, since that very first day...

CURTIS is available now at all retailers

DEAD HEAT RANCH
Boots Optional
Betting on Grace
Overnight Love

DEVIL'S BEND
Chasing Dreams
Vanishing Dreams

MISPLACED HALOS
Protected in Darkness
Salvation in Darkness
Bound in Darkness

OFFICE INTRIGUE
Office Intrigue
Intrigued Out of the Office
Their Rebellious Submissive
Their Famous Dominant
Their Ruthless Sadist
Their Naughty Student
Their Fairy Princess

PIER 70
Reckless
Fearless
Speechless
Harmless
Clueless

SNIPER 1 SECURITY
Wait for Morning
Never Say Never
Tomorrow's Too Late

SOUTHERN BOY MAFIA/DEVIL'S PLAYGROUND
Beautifully Brutal
Without Regret
Beautifully Loyal
Without Restraint